THE FURTHER ~~ADVENTURES~~
OF GOBBOL~~INO~~
THE LITTLE WOODEN HORSE

URSULA MORAY WILLIAMS

Illustrated by Pauline Baynes

PUFFIN BOOKS

For Alexandra

Puffin Books, Penguin Books Ltd, Harmondsworth, Middlesex, England
Viking Penguin Inc., 40 West 23rd Street, New York, New York 10010, U.S.A.
Penguin Books Australia Ltd, Ringwood, Victoria, Australia
Penguin Books Canada Limited, 2801 John Street, Markham, Ontario, Canada L3R 1B4
Penguin Books (N.Z.) Ltd, 182-190 Wairau Road, Auckland 10, New Zealand

First published 1984
Reprinted 1986
Copyright © Ursula Moray Williams, 1984
Illustrations copyright © Pauline Baynes, 1984
All rights reserved

Made and printed in Great Britain by
Richard Clay (The Chaucer Press) Ltd,
Bungay, Suffolk
Set in 12 on 14 pt Baskerville

CONTENTS

CHAPTER 1

A MESSAGE FOR GOBBOLINO

ONE evening in late summer, Gobbolino the kitchen cat was basking on the steps of his happy home, and thinking how lucky he was to have arrived in such agreeable surroundings after all the adventures that had befallen him as a witch's kitten.

'And I hardly deserve it,' thought little Gobbolino, 'for I was born and bred and brought up in the cavern of a witch. My little sister Sootica was happy enough learning to make wicked spells, and inventing naughty tricks to play on people. I wonder what has become of her now?'

He could hardly remember his mother, Grimalkin, but his sister had once been dear to his heart, and he could not help thinking of her now and again. True, she had teased and scoffed at him and called him all kinds of unkind names, but in the end she had saved his life when the witch wanted to get rid of him, and he hoped she had not suffered for it on his account.

While he lay drowsing in the sun the farm children were busy at their tasks on the farm. The girls were helping their mother in the dairy, making butter, skimming the cream and scalding the shining pans. The boys were working in the fields with their father, and presently everyone would come home to tea in the farmhouse, where nobody would pass him by without a kindly word or a chuck under the chin. It was a happy life for a kitchen cat, and Gobbolino expected it to last for ever.

Presently twilight fell, and the farmer's wife closed the dairy doors. She and her daughters, tired but contented, clattered across the yard to the kitchen, carrying jugs of cream and milk.

Down in the fields, gates were opening and shutting, horses' hooves were stamping, and the iron-rimmed wheels of the haycarts could be heard grinding across the stones of the farm lane. Now the finished hayricks would be standing like sentinels at the edge of the fields – food for the cattle in the long winter days to come. The farmer and his boys were trudging home to tea, content that life was mainly as it should be, and that the last of the hay was cut and stacked.

They stabled the horses and tramped into the house, stopping for a moment to say a friendly word to Gobbolino, who would only wait a very few minutes before he followed them into the kitchen. He knew there would be a saucer of milk set down for him at the fireside, and when it was finished he might choose any lap he liked to sit on, for the rest of the evening.

But as the rim of the sun dipped behind the far-off purple mountains, a large owl flew silently up the lane and dropped a leaf on the farmhouse steps, close to Gobbolino's feet.

In a minute the owl was gone, but the leaf flapped a little in the soft evening breeze, and came to rest by his paw. Even a moving shadow tempts a cat to chase it, so Gobbolino raised a forefoot and brought it down smartly on top of the leaf.

A flight of wild geese from the river below the farm flew over his head, uttering their strange cries. Gobbolino ducked with his ears pressed close against his head, and when they were gone the leaf had fluttered halfway across the yard and was still flapping. Gobbolino got up to follow it, but voices called him from the kitchen door:

'Gobbolino! Gobbolino! It is supper-time and your milk is ready by the fire! Where are you, Gobbolino?'

Gobbolino trotted indoors.

His milk was warm and fresh as usual. The fire was hot and glowing. When the family had finished eating he waited until the farmer's wife sat down with her knitting, for the children were so restless he seldom got half an hour in peace upon their knees. While she cleared the table and washed the dishes he took a last, short stroll outside, and found that a great harvest moon had risen over the farmyard, making a new, white world of the barns and the strawstacks and the stables and the wagons quietly ranged beside the pond.

Halfway across the yard the leaf still lay, motionless now, because the breeze had followed the sun behind the hills to rest.

Gobbolino walked across the yard and sniffed at the leaf, not so much from curiosity but because it stood out in the moonlight like a finger that beckoned, spoiling the lovely quiet carpet of light spread out in front of him.

As he lifted a paw to flatten the leaf against the earth, the moonlight shone upon a number of words written across the leaf, a sight that Gobbolino found exceptionally strange, since leaves fall off trees, and do not provide sheets of writing paper any more than trees provide writing tables in their native state. He held down the leaf with his forepaw and carefully read the inscription upon it.

When he had made out the meaning of the words written there he nearly fell over backwards in his astonishment, and for a moment his heart almost stopped beating. He raised his paw for the briefest second and the leaf fluttered away from him, stirred by the very last echo of the evening breeze. It disappeared underneath the chicken house.

Gobbolino found it after a while, among the shadows. Holding it very firmly this time he read aloud:

'PLEASE COME AND HELP ME, BROTHER! OH PLEASE DO! OH DO! DO!'

It was such an extraordinary message to be written on a leaf. And it was such an extraordinary message for a kitchen cat to receive! Gobbolino did not know what to make of it.

There was only one person in the world who had the right to call him brother, and that was his little sister Sootica, who was a witch's cat.

Long ago Gobbolino had been a witch's cat himself, until he was saved by a spell, and became what he had always longed to be, an ordinary kitchen cat with a home of his own and a coat that was almost tabby.

Nobody really liked witches' cats, or wanted them at their firesides. The farmer and his wife did not like them Gobbolino remembered the day, now long ago, when they had turned him out into the wide world to fend for himself because he had blown sparks out of his ears, and turned himself into all kinds of grotesque shapes and sizes to make the children laugh.

As he remembered those far-off days the old sensation of loneliness and not being wanted came back to him, and he shivered in the moonlight at the thought of his little sister Sootica feeling wretched and unhappy too, far up there in the Hurricane Mountains, or wherever else she might be now. And yet . . . his sister Sootica had been glad to be a witch's cat. Over and over again she had told him of her ambitions to know the book of magic by heart, to cast spells over people, and to fly down the night on a broomstick, making people cringe and shiver. She hoped to be the most famous witch's cat in all the world!

What could have happened to make her call for help in this manner? Was it possible that the witch had punished her with some dreadful revenge because she had rescued Gobbolino when he was about to be flung down the Hurricane Mountains? And because he owed her his life ought he not to help her when she called out to him?

But where could she be now? *Where?*

The owl never came back.

Gobbolino waited outside in the yard until the children came and chased him indoors.

'The hobgoblins will get you!' they teased him, spreading out his blanket beside the fire.

But all night long Sootica's message to him rang in his ears: 'PLEASE COME AND HELP ME, BROTHER! OH PLEASE DO! OH DO! DO!'

CHAPTER 2

THE LITTLE WOODEN HORSE

BY morning Gobbolino had not slept a wink all night. He tried to tell himself that the message was perhaps a trick to get him back into the witch's cave and make him a slave again, but in his heart of hearts he knew this was not true. Witches did not want ordinary cats in their homes any more than ordinary people wanted witches' cats, and she would be glad to get rid of him.

Besides, there was something so beseeching, so pleading in the message scrawled on the leaf that he felt it could only have come from his sister Sootica. And just as she had helped him before so he must help her now.

It broke his heart to leave the farmhouse and the kind family without a word of explanation, but he was afraid that if he stopped to explain his mission they would either prevent him from going, or, worse still, they would refuse to have him back again, because his sister was a witch, and with all his heart he counted on a welcome and his usual place by the fire when he came home.

He had made it his duty to watch the baby asleep in its basket under the apple trees, and again he was overcome with remorse at leaving his post. But one of the farm dogs, who was too old to go into the fields, kindly agreed to take his place, and just as the clock was striking seven in the morning Gobbolino crept out of the orchard, across the yard and away from the farm.

For the first mile he felt so lonely that half a dozen times he nearly turned back. It was so long since he had travelled all by himself. The happy bustle of the farm-house, inside and out, had become so much a part of his new life that he did not realize how much he would miss it

'But I shall soon be back again,' Gobbolino comforted himself. 'I don't know what I can do to help my sister, but once I see her I shall find out, and then I shall come home.'

He set his face towards the Hurricane Mountains, because that was the only place he knew where his sister Sootica might be, and thinking, as he did, that every hour was bringing them closer together he began to feel much more cheerful, and even to purr a little as he trotted along.

'For I am such a lucky cat!' his heart sang. 'I have a home to come back to, and kind friends to welcome me on my return. The children will be a little sad waiting for me and wondering when I am coming home, but when I do return they will be very happy, and every-thing will be as it was before.'

The mountains were a great way off, and although Gobbolino walked all day they did not seem to come any nearer. He drank at a stream, but had had nothing to eat since leaving the farm, and his paws were so sore he could hardly stand up on them. Every now and again he stopped to give each of them a good lick, and to clean out the dust and grit from between his pads. This refreshed him a little, but he thought very anxiously about the next day and the next, and the terribly long distance he would have to walk before he reached the far-off Hurricane Mountains.

At last the road ran into a forest, and here the going was easier, because the pine needles made a carpet quite springy and pleasant to walk upon.

Gobbolino was trotting along quite happily when he came upon a little wooden horse grazing in a small green glade.

They greeted one another very civilly. Gobbolino was delighted to find someone he could talk to for a little

while, but he wished he were able to enjoy the berries that the little wooden horse was helping himself to from the bushes round the glade. Gobbolino noticed that he kept removing his head and putting them through the hole into his wooden body.

'Are those berries good to eat?' he asked the little wooden horse.

'Why yes! they are very good indeed!' said the little wooden horse. 'But I am not picking them for myself. I am picking them for my mistress, the wife of my dear master, Uncle Peder the toy-maker, who lives close by, and she will turn them into jam, and put them into little pies, and bottle what is left over for the winter.'

'Did you say you lived close by?' said Gobbolino eagerly. 'Do you think your master has a shed where I could spend the night, and maybe catch a mouse or two for my supper? Because I still have a long way to go,' he added, 'and I have had nothing to eat all day.'

'Why! you must come home with me at once!' said the little wooden horse. 'My missus will give you something nice to eat and a comfortable bed for the night. Follow me!'

He set out at such a pace on his twinkling wooden legs, with his wooden wheels spinning round like tops, that Gobbolino could only limp after him, losing distance all the way.

When the little wooden horse saw how he was faltering he came cantering back and exclaimed in sympathy:

'Why! You are quite lame! You must have blisters on all four of your feet! Jump on my back, and I will take you to my home!'

Gobbolino was only too grateful to jump on to the wooden back of his kind friend. He saw how strong was the little wooden horse, and how well made. His stripes were blue and freshly painted. His saddle was red and his spots were black, yet there was nothing brand-new about him. He seemed wise and good and kind, as if he had been around some time in the world, and Gobbolino wondered very much how he came to be in this wood, and what was his story.

But before he could ask him any questions they arrived at a little house in the middle of the forest. It was built with white walls, a green painted door, and there was a pretty dovecot in the garden.

The little wooden horse trotted through the garden gate and deposited Gobbolino at the door, which he then pushed open with his wooden wheels, and led the cat inside.

A rosy-faced old woman was cooking at the kitchen stove, and from her cooking came the most delicious flavoursome smells.

Gobbolino had not intended to go into the house. He meant to find a corner where he could spend the night in the garden. But the little wooden horse was blocking the doorway, and before he could escape the old woman had turned round.

'Well I never!' she exclaimed in surprise. 'Whatever have we got here now? What a handsome cat! What lovely dark fur, and what beautiful blue eyes! Wherever did you find him?'

The little wooden horse was explaining how they had come across each other while picking blackberries in the

forest, but at that moment the door behind them gave way to a tall, handsome old man who at once took the little wooden horse's head in his hands and began to rub it very affectionately.

Before many minutes had passed Gobbolino found himself lapping a saucer of rich yellow milk, while a comfortable cushion awaited his tired feet. Kind hands brushed and combed his fur and, while the old woman disposed of the berries the little wooden horse had picked in the glade, Gobbolino fell fast asleep, lulled by the bubbling of the pot and the crackling of the fire.

He slept so soundly that he did not wake up all night. When he opened his eyes it was morning, and there was nobody in the kitchen but himself and the little old woman.

She was just as kind to him as she had been the night before, and, when he went into the garden to find his friend the little wooden horse, she explained to him that the horse had gone off with his master, Uncle Peder, to take some toys to a far-off customer, and they would not be home until nightfall.

Gobbolino was very disappointed, for he wanted to say good-bye and to thank the little wooden horse before he went on his journey, but he knew he ought to leave early if he was to get well on his way to the Hurricane Mountains before dark.

He explained this to the old woman, who looked disappointed in her turn.

'I thought you were coming to live with us!' she said reproachfully. 'Why are you in such a hurry to get to the Hurricane Mountains?'

Gobbolino began to tell her his story.

'I have a good home of my own to return to,' he explained, 'but I have a little sister high up in the mountains, who belongs to a witch. I am afraid she may be in some kind of trouble, because she sent me a message to come and help her, and that is where I am going. I am truly grateful, ma'am, for your hospitality, and I so badly wanted to say good-bye to my friend the little wooden horse before I left.'

But the old woman was looking at him with horror in her face.

'Your sister is a *witch's* cat?' she exclaimed. 'Then what are you?'

'I am a kitchen cat!' said Gobbolino simply, but she turned away and began to make such a clatter with the pots and pans that he felt sure she did not believe him. He crept into a corner of the kitchen and tears of shame filled his beautiful blue eyes. He was afraid that if he left the house now his friend the wooden horse would get into trouble for bringing a witch's cat into the house. Twice he left the kitchen and trotted out through the garden gate, but twice he came back again. His paws, too, were so sore he realized he would not be able to go far without another day's rest, so he crept into a little potting shed in the garden and waited until he could tell the whole of his story to the little wooden horse.

Late in the afternoon Uncle Peder and the wooden horse returned. Gobbolino was about to run out and greet them, but he saw the old woman in the doorway, and he did not want to run the risk of being sent away without an explanation.

So he crouched in the shed, and heard his wooden friend inquiring anxiously where the cat was, and whether his paws had healed during the day.

'Why, I have no idea where your friend the cat is,' said the old woman testily. 'I haven't seen it since breakfast-time this morning. And a fine trick you played on me!' she added, rounding on the little wooden horse. 'It is just a bold, wicked witch's cat, off to join its sister witch in the Hurricane Mountains! We don't want that sort of thing here!'

'I can't believe such a story!' said Uncle Peder in astonishment. 'That was a *good* cat if ever I saw one! Remember, wife, you made a mistake once before, and it is quite possible to make one again!'

'Oh dear! Oh dear! How hasty I am!' lamented the old woman, remembering the time, long ago, when she had chased away the little wooden horse from her door. 'Well you may be right, Uncle Peder, and I am wrong . . . but the creature told me himself that his sister was a witch's cat, and what does that make him himself I should like to know?'

Gobbolino stole out of the potting shed and into the kitchen. He sat down beside the little wooden horse and told his whole story to the family.

The old woman was ashamed that she had not listened to him before. She gave him an excellent dinner, and began to put scraps of food into a little bag for him on his journey to the mountains.

'I must set off immediately,' Gobbolino said in some anxiety, 'because I have wasted a whole day, and my sister must be desperate to know if I am coming.'

'You can't go into the forest by night!' the little wooden horse said. 'It is very dangerous, and you could lose your way. Wait until first light in the morning, and then I will go with you as far as the open plain, and see you on your journey.'

Having heard his story Uncle Peder and the old woman were quite agreed that the little wooden horse should go a short way with him and see him on his journey, especially since Gobbolino's paws were by no means healed, and he had many miles to travel before he came to the Hurricane Mountains.

'But come back to us as soon as you have seen your friend on his way!' they told the little wooden horse. 'Because if anything happened to you it would break our hearts. We could not possibly go on living without you now!'

Gobbolino and the little wooden horse lay down together beside the fire and slept till early dawn. Then they each took a bag of food that the old woman had prepared for them and set out into the forest, with the early morning awakening all around them, bird calls, spiders' threads, little gold dawn clouds in the sky above, and mists weaving and waving between the distant trees.

Gobbolino hopped along on his healing feet, using three paws at a time to rest the other, until the wooden horse persuaded him to ride while he could, and save himself for the rougher roads when he would have no one to help him.

CHAPTER 3

THE OWL

SEVERAL times during the day Gobbolino begged the little wooden horse to set him down and go back to Uncle Peder and his wife, but the horse only said:

'Wait a little! Only just a little while longer and we shall have come to the end of the forest. I will go home then.'

At last it seemed that the trees were thinning out, and the dense woods were coming to an end.

But the light that was filtering through the branches was less bright, because the sun had gone behind the clouds, and it became quite obvious that a large storm was blowing up in the sky.

'Now isn't that tiresome!' said the little wooden horse. 'While we were deep inside the forest it couldn't have harmed us very much, but now that the trees are thinner there is no shelter and nowhere to hide ourselves. We shall just have to make up our minds to get soaking wet until the storm is over.'

Beyond the trees the landscape spread far out across meadows and valleys, and still infinitely distant appeared the ramparts of the Hurricane Mountains, now shrouded in a pall of driving rain.

'I thought we must be nearly there!' said Gobbolino sorrowfully. 'They look every bit as far away as when I first left home. And just suppose, when I arrive there, I find my sister is not there at all? Whatever shall I do?'

They both realized that besides the rain, night was now falling, and as the darkness slowly enveloped them they could not tell if it were stormclouds or evening that was stealing the daylight out of the sky.

The rainclouds dallied over the meadows, but a few heavy drops spattered Gobbolino and the little wooden horse huddling together under a tree.

Suddenly Gobbolino became aware of a large owl sitting above them on a branch, looking at them very seriously out of round amber eyes, which it closed the moment they looked back at it.

Remembering the owl who had brought him his sister's message he stood on his hind legs with his paws reaching up the bole of the tree, while he begged the owl to tell him if he really were the same bird or quite a different one.

The owl took absolutely no notice of him. If anything it closed its eyes rather tighter than before.

It must be quite another owl, Gobbolino thought, but on the other hand, owls flew far and wide, and knew a great deal about the goings-on in field and forest, and in the district round them.

'Sir Owl!' Gobbolino called politely. 'Please can you tell me one thing? Do you know whether a witch still lives in the Hurricane Mountains, in a cavern right at the top?'

The owl's great amber eyes opened wide for a moment, and then shut up tightly, like boxes.

'Oh please, please tell me, sir Owl,' Gobbolino pleaded. 'It is so very important to me to know if there is a cavern up there still lived in by a witch! Please tell me if you can! Please do!'

The owl gave the faintest nod of its head, although its eyes remained tightly closed.

'And does the witch have a cat?' asked Gobbolino, trembling with excitement.

This time the owl's nod was so faint that he looked down at the wooden horse in perplexity.

'It said "yes"!' said the little wooden horse quite positively. 'But I think you forgot to say "Thank you!"'

'Oh thank you! Thank you, kind Owl!' said Gobbolino, much abashed. 'And please, sir, please will you tell me . . . does the cat have a name? And can you tell me if that name could be Sootica?'

At that, the owl gave such a loud screech that both the friends were startled. Gobbolino fell backwards from the tree, and at the same moment the owl left the branch above and sailed away into the darkness.

The single drops of rain became a downpour that battered the scanty branches and fell upon their heads like wet pebbles. The little wooden horse turned his head towards the tree and told Gobbolino to crouch underneath his wooden body, but there was not much protection there. In his turn Gobbolino tried to shroud the little wooden horse in his fur.

'How ashamed I am at bringing you so far from your home!' Gobbolino said. 'You could be warm and comfortable beside your own kitchen fire if you had not chosen to come and help me find my little sister. First thing in the morning you must go home, for I can see my way now as far as the mountains, and when the storm is over and the daylight comes I can find the road to them alone.'

'We will see about that,' said the little wooden horse, 'but just remember, I came of my own accord. You have nothing to feel ashamed about.'

It became so dark that they could no longer see each other, but Gobbolino knew his friend was there by the feel of his strong and sturdy legs, and the four wooden wheels at the ends of them, while the little wooden horse could feel Gobbolino's soft coat until the rain turned it into a soaking wet blanket that dripped wet on to the earth around them.

Above them the storm roared and raged till they seemed surrounded by clamour and the relentless sweep of the drenching rain.

Suddenly the noise became much fainter, and then ceased. At the same time something like a thick, soft ciderdown descended gently on top of them, wrapping them closely and blotting out the sound of the storm. Their cold wet bodies began to glow with warmth and dry themselves, their feet felt warm and cosy, and they sank gratefully into the soft feathers of the owl's wings spread over the pair of them, to dry and comfort them during the night.

CHAPTER 4

THE CHASE

THEY awoke to bright sunlight. The owl was gone, leaving them warm and dry.

Gobbolino's fur shone like silk, while the paint on the little wooden horse gleamed as if it had just been polished.

The Hurricane Mountains were clean and blue in the morning light. They did not look so far away after all.

'Why! I shall get there by the evening!' said Gobbolino joyously. 'Now you can go home again, my kind friend, because I really cannot accept your kindness any longer. You can be quite certain that by this time tomorrow I will have found my little sister Sootica!'

The little wooden horse looked doubtful.

'And what then?' he said. 'After such a long journey you will be much too tired to confront the witch or any other danger that may threaten her. While I am beside you, you can ride on my back and keep your strength for any adventures still to come. I will go just a little further with you before I turn back.'

Gobbolino could only be grateful, as much for his company as for his help and kindness. His paws were nearly healed, and since there was no sign of the owl, they left the forest and stepped out across the vast plateau of fields and meadows towards the mountains.

They were very glad of the food that the old woman had given them for their journey, and they had catcn their dinner beside a little stream in the middle of the plain when Gobbolino raised his head and exclaimed, 'What is that strange noise I can hear?'

The little wooden horse listened too, but the noise had died away, and they finished their meal.

Gobbolino heard it again.

'There! Far away to the west of us! It sounds like wild birds crying, only different . . . quite different! Don't you hear it yourself?'

The little wooden horse did hear it. He raised his wooden head and sniffed the air.

'I can hear it!' he said. 'And I think we ought to go back to the forest as quickly as we can!'

'*What?*' exclaimed Gobbolino in horror. 'When we have come so far? Just look what a long way behind us the trees are! Why! we are more than halfway to the mountains already. Don't let's go back! Let's go on as quickly as we can!'

The sound had ceased. The little wooden horse jumped to his feet and stood looking westward with his ears pricked.

'I think we should go back to the forest!' he repeated solemnly.

Gobbolino looked at him in astonishment.

'What are you afraid of?' he asked. 'How can wild birds hurt us . . . if it is wild birds?'

'Supposing it isn't wild birds!' said the little wooden horse. 'Supposing it is . . . *wild* . . . *things*!'

'Not wild beasts?' said Gobbolino. 'How could it

possibly be? Not lions! Not tigers nor hyenas! Not leopards! And wolves hunt in the forests, yet you want us to go back there!'

'Dogs!' said the little wooden horse flatly.

'Dogs?' screeched Gobbolino jumping three feet into the air.

'Hounds . . .! On the scent . . .' said the little wooden horse. 'I don't know what scent . . . but if they smell us it could be us. Jump on my back and see if you can tell me which way they are coming.'

Gobbolino jumped on to the back of the little wooden horse, standing up as high on his hind legs as he could stretch himself. But far as he could view across the western plain there was nothing threatening in the landscape, and the noise of the baying had quite died away and disappeared.

'I dare say they are not coming in this direction after all!' said the little wooden horse, much relieved.

'Then we can go on!' said Gobbolino happily.

'I still think we should go back and wait till evening,' said the little wooden horse. 'By then the hounds will have gone home, and we can travel quite easily out in the open. There will be some moonlight presently to help us.'

'But we shall have lost so much time!' wailed Gobbolino. 'We ought to be in the mountains by sundown, and if we go back we won't be there till late tomorrow. Let's wait a little while and listen, and if they come no nearer we can go on our way!'

Together they crouched down by the stream where they had eaten their dinner, listening to every sound that came across the plain – the trilling of the larks above, the sizzling of the crickets, the babble of the water and the spasmodic chirp of a water bird. There was no other sound at all.

'We must go on!' said Gobbolino. 'Every minute is important if I am to reach the mountains before the sun sets.'

The little wooden horse still hesitated.

'This is where we must part, my kind little friend!' said Gobbolino. 'I will go on to the mountains and you must go home. We will both be well on our separate journeys before dark. I have so much to thank you for, and I cannot accept any more of your kindness or your companionship. It is time that we said good-bye.'

The little wooden horse looked very unhappy, shifting from one wooden leg to the other.

'I would gladly go further with you,' he said at last, 'but I have such a very strong feeling that we ought both to go back to the forest and wait till evening.'

'I can't see any reason for it!' said Gobbolino pettishly. 'All those miles backwards when we could be going forwards? How can you think of such a thing? Go back by all means, my dear faithful friend, but don't ask me to come too until I have found my sister and heard what she wants of me. How can you possibly think of asking me to turn my back on the mountains now?'

The little wooden horse began to paw the ground in an agony of embarrassment and distress. When he saw that nothing he said would move Gobbolino he bowed his wooden head and said very sadly:

'Very well, my friend, we will do as you say! I will go

home to my dear old master and missus, who need me even more than you do, and I will wish you the very best of luck on your journey, and protection from every danger. For I am very much afraid there *will* be danger!' the little wooden horse said sadly, but Gobbolino only tossed his head, while a spark of bravado flashed in his beautiful blue eyes as he exclaimed, 'Danger? Why! Haven't I met danger before? Haven't I confronted witches and spells and wicked enchantments, and been flown away with on a broomstick and dropped in a raging river? Do you think I am afraid of danger, my little wooden friend? Not I!'

But the little wooden horse was looking forwards across the plain, not north to the Hurricane Mountains. His wooden ears were pricked and listening, although no sound came but the flutter of the wind in the grass, the trilling of the larks, the sizzling of the crickets, the babble of the water, and now and again the sudden chirp downstream of a water bird.

'Good-bye, Gobbolino!' he said quietly. 'May your journey be successful, and I hope you will soon find your sister. I shall watch every day for your return once you have helped her. Be sure you come by the cottage on your journey home, and tell us all your adventures. Good-bye!'

There were tears in the eyes of the little wooden horse, and Gobbolino was crying too. He thanked his friend over and over again for his companionship, assuring him that he would never have come as far as this if he had not had his help, and been able to rest his blistered paws by riding on the horse's back.

Very sadly they climbed up opposite sides of the stream, and set off, one northwards to the mountains, and the other southwards to the forest and home. Every now and again they turned and waved to one another until the tall grasses enveloped them, and the great vast plain seemed as empty as if it had swallowed up the pair of them.

Gobbolino felt terribly lonely, but nothing would have persuaded him to retrace his footsteps, and with every pace forward he congratulated himself on getting nearer and nearer to his goal.

'How could I possibly have gone back to the forest?' he asked himself. 'My sister will be counting the minutes till I arrive, and already she will be wondering why I have not come sooner!'

He had trotted on for more than an hour, and had made a wide circle to avoid one of the few farms and villages that were dotted about the plain, when he heard again the strange sound that had so disturbed the senses of the little wooden horse.

From the far westward came the cry of hounds moving up the plain, a long protracted baying that could no longer be confused with the cry of geese, or of any other bird. It was unmistakably the baying of a pack of hounds.

Gobbolino's heart began to thump. At the same time he quickened his pace, hurrying along on his four paws that were once more sore and aching. The noise was a great distance off, and no doubt the hounds were after their own quarry, and had nothing to do with him at all, but they were closer than they had been when the two friends ate their dinner beside the stream, and it was quite possible that they were coming back to their kennels in the village and might cross his trail.

Gobbolino began to gallop, the little bag of food bouncing up and down under his chin. It became such a burden that he threw it away, and was able to run faster without it, but the baying of the hounds came nearer.

The pack was sweeping up the plain now, and Gobbolino realized at last the honest fears of the little wooden horse, for there was not a rock, not a tree where he could hide himself until they passed. He turned his face towards the village, hoping he might reach it in time to find a shed or a shelter of some kind before the hounds overtook him. He tried not to think of other dangers like watchdogs or youths with sticks, or stones being thrown at him, or similar dangers. The threat behind him was quite enough to concentrate on while he was running.

He galloped along gasping with terror, and now it seemed almost certain that the hounds had found his trail, for the baying grew louder and louder and more terrifying the faster he ran.

And another sound had joined them – a rattling, clattering noise that pursued him and came closer and closer, with snorts and blowings and the thunder of spinning wooden wheels.

Gobbolino was about to fall flat on his face from sheer terror when a familiar voice panted in his ear, 'Jump on my back, Gobbolino! Don't stop for a moment! Jump, I tell you! Jump!'

The little wooden horse overtook him at full gallop, and with a desperate leap Gobbolino gained the painted

saddle and they tore on, clinging together as the horse's wooden wheels spun and clattered across the plain.

The hounds were not far behind them, and the baying was terrible. It was quite obvious that they had picked up Gobbolino's scent and were following it in full cry.

But all of a sudden the baying died down, as if the pack had stopped for a moment, or overrun the trail. They seemed to be casting about to find it again, uttering little whimpers and false cries before returning to the same place again, and once more becoming bewildered and more and more defeated. This happened at the point where Gobbolino jumped on to the back of the little wooden horse, and his scent gave place to the trail of wooden wheels. For a short time it seemed as if the two friends had escaped from their pursuers.

Then the hounds realized that the scent they were following was mingled with the smell of wood and paint. It was still there, though faint and uncertain. All they had to do was to follow the new smell of paint and wood, and with a united howl of delight they set off again.

Now, although the little wooden horse sped like a streak of lightning, the hounds were gaining on him fast.

'Put me down and let me run!' Gobbolino pleaded, for he felt sure his weight was holding back the speed of the little wooden horse, but even side by side they could not outpace the pack of hounds.

When both were at the end of their strength and about to turn and face the baying pack, they arrived suddenly at the gate of an ancient church, and slipping quickly through the lych-gate, arrived inside the churchyard.

CHAPTER 5

SANCTUARY IN
THE HAUNTED CHURCH

An old priest came from the doorway of the church and walked down the path of the churchyard.

Gobbolino and the little wooden horse flew to hide themselves in the folds of his cassock, as a last and desperate refuge from the hounds, but to their amazement the pack stopped short at the lych-gate. One or two jumped over the wall and ran about among the tombstones, but they seemed very uneasy, and took no further notice of their prey.

The next moment a fearful clanging of bells in every discord burst out of the belfry above their heads. The old priest flinched, closed his eyes and crossed himself. A crowd of terrified bats flew out of the tower, and every hound turned tail and fled, howling. They could be heard retreating, still howling, across the plain, until they had run quite out of earshot.

The old priest stooped down, and gently stroking Gobbolino murmured:

'Ah, my little cat! For once the haunted church has stood you in good stead, for I think it has saved your life!'

While they had been running for their lives the first shades of evening had crept across the plain, and were mingling with the pink glow on the peaks of the Hurricane Mountains.

At first Gobbolino and the little wooden horse were too shaken and breathless to tell their story to the priest, but as they recovered their breath they asked him if they might have sanctuary in the church overnight.

'Sanctuary!' exclaimed the priest. 'Yes, of course you may have sanctuary! But I doubt if any of my parishioners would call it that! The church is haunted. You heard for yourselves the terrible clamour of the bells, though nobody rings them! The bell-ringers refuse to come any more. The choir won't sing, in case it happens in the middle of a service. Nobody will clean the church, because the cleaners are so frightened. And I no longer have any congregation to preach to. It is no wonder they won't sit in the pews because the place is so neglected and dirty.'

Gobbolino and the little wooden horse explained their plight, and the priest gave them all the comfort and sympathy in his power.

'I would invite you to spend the night in my house,' he said, 'but my housekeeper does not like animals in the house. But I know she will give me some food for you, and at least you will be safe and dry, whether you sleep in the vestry or in the pulpit. Bless you both – I wish you well!'

The priest went away, and soon returned with a bowl of warm bread and milk which the two of them gladly shared.

Then he blessed them again, adding sadly:

'Not all my blessings seem able to rid the church of its haunting, nor all my prayers. All my life I have believed that Good is stronger than Evil, but in this case there seems to be nothing that I can do about it. Take as little notice as you can of the haunting bells, and sleep in peace!'

The priest went home to bed, while the little wooden horse and Gobbolino explored the old church, which was very beautiful, but dirty with bat droppings and months of neglect.

The bats themselves kept up a constant whirring of wings as they came back into the church tower from the churchyard, where the baying of the hounds had driven them. They disappeared inside the bell tower, having, it seemed, no particular fear of ghosts.

Gobbolino remembered bats from his life in the witch's cave. He did not care for them very much, but he looked on them as harmless. A clinging suspicion that the hounds might come back that way made the friends decide not to sleep in the body of the church. When they had finished their bread and milk they climbed up the winding stair to the bell tower and saw hundreds of bats clinging to the bell-ropes, with their wings folded one across the other. They did not seem to worry about ghosts.

It was warmer up here than down below. Gobbolino and the little wooden horse found a comfortable alcove halfway up the stairs, and were thankful to rest their legs, and to warm themselves a little in the last rays of the sun pouring through a niche in the side of the tower.

Presently they became aware of a rustling and a whispering. The bats were waking up and peering at them.

'Who are you? Where are you from? Did you come with those horrible howling dogs? And if so, why did they leave you behind?' Their eager little heads were peering forward and their bright eyes twinkled at Gobbolino and the little wooden horse.

These began to tell them their story, but they had hardly begun before a bat perched on the biggest of the bells called out:

'The sun has touched the rim of the bell, brothers! It is time to get up! Now! Now!'

Suddenly, with the most fearful clamour every bat

left the bell-ropes at once, and dived below into the
body of the church. Some of them slipped through cracks
into the churchyard outside. but the rest of them joined
in a mad chase round and round the nave and the
aisles, in and out of the screen, up and over the organ, in
and out of the pulpit, while above them and around
them the clamour of the liberated bells filled every
corner of the building and echoed far beyond the priest's
house, the churchyard and the village.

It all happened so suddenly that Gobbolino and the little wooden horse were taken by surprise.

They cowered in their alcove, quite overwhelmed by the dreadful noise and the flurry of the whirling black bodies streaming past them. They could well understand the horror of the village, and the unwillingness of the congregation to enter the church. The bells took a long time to calm down after such agitation.

There was nothing they could do to calm the mad ecstasy of the bats, and they were so tired that all they desired was a little peace and quiet to sleep the night away after their adventure.

Peace they had at last, once they became used to the constant whirling of the bats, which was, after all, rather like the noise of the wind in the trees on a stormy night.

They slept, in spite of their exhaustion, with one ear open, expecting the same blast of bells when the bats should have finished their cavorting and come back to their perches at daybreak. But to their surprise they returned quietly, taking up their places one by one, and clinging like moths to the bell-ropes, till the whole tower seemed to be draped in velvet columns.

When he thought they were all assembled, and before they closed their eyes, Gobbolino addressed them, in the pale dawn light that was filling the belfry.

'Gentlemen!' Gobbolino said. 'I have something to say to you! Do you realize how much trouble you are causing in this fine old church by the way you are behaving? Everybody thinks the place is haunted!'

'It's our home!' whined some of the bats.

Others murmured, 'We don't like the bells any more than you do! Some day perhaps they will fall down and then we can live here in peace and quiet!'

'How can you speak like that?' said Gobbolino, shocked. 'The place is so dirty, and everybody hates you, apart from the haunting. Once they find out who is ringing the bells I wouldn't give much for your chances! They'll smoke you out, I wouldn't be surprised!'

'Oh! Oh!' raged the bats. 'And who is going to tell them? What business is it of yours anyway? We already have the old priest preaching at us, and it makes us feel most uncomfortable! We don't want to stay in his old church, but we haven't anywhere else to go.'

'Turn them out of the belfry! We don't want them in here!' called out more bats.

'The church is a sanctuary!' other bats reproved them. 'We are not allowed to turn them out.'

They began to whisper among themselves.

'Wait until they leave of their own accord, and then we'll set upon them!' Gobbolino distinctly heard them say.

He and the little wooden horse looked at one another.

They had planned to leave first thing in the morning, but to be attacked by the bats would be just as bad as being chased by the hounds. The alternative was to stay inside the church. And of what use was safety if they were in prison?

The little wooden horse shook his head in perplexity. He felt brave enough to take on any number of bats, and his wooden body would not suffer much harm from their scratches and bites, but he was afraid Gobbolino would come off very badly if a lot of the creatures attacked him at once, and he stood thinking in some dejection of what to do next.

Suddenly he heard Gobbolino speak, and at once every bat in the belfry stopped squeaking and pricked up its ears and listened.

'Gentlemen!' Gobbolino said. 'I have something to propose to you. But please tell me first: are you happy in this place, or would you prefer to have another home?'

'Why, yes we would!' said the bats complainingly. 'It is noisy here! It is crowded – we hardly have enough room to sleep in, all on top of one another like that, and the bells make a hideous noise if we turn over. Of course we would rather have another home!'

'Ah!' said Gobbolino wisely.

'But there are so many of us it is quite hopeless to think of finding one!' the bats continued. 'And we don't want to split up our families. We've got grannies and great-grandpas and great-great-aunties and all kinds of ancestors as well as little nieces and nephews, and lots of babies. We all want to live together, and where would we find enough room except in a belfry?'

'Ah!' said Gobbolino again, very wisely.

'Why? Do you know of anywhere?' the bats asked, all agog with interest and excitement.

'I do!' replied Gobbolino. 'Up in the Hurricane Mountains where I used to live there are hundreds and hundreds of empty caves. I was born in one and I know. There is room there for thousands of bats! There are no church bells and nobody comes and tells you to go away. Every family could have its own cave . . . every family!'

By now the bats were shimmering and wriggling with anticipation.

'Are you sure? Do you promise?' they asked Gobbolino, beginning to leave the bell-ropes and to fly round the belfry, not all at once, but in ones and twos so that the hideous clash of bells did not occur.

'I am sure! And I promise!' said Gobbolino solemnly. 'But you must go and take possession in an orderly fashion, because a witch lives in the highest cave, and you don't want to annoy her or she might turn you into something horrid. Leave this place two by two, and fly straight up to the mountains. You have only to come back here if you find I am not telling you the truth.'

'But they won't come back, because I *am* telling them the truth!' said Gobbolino, as two by two and quite quietly the bats left the ropes, flew out of the tower, and vanished in the early dawn towards the Hurricane Mountains.

Gobbolino stopped the very last pair as they were leaving.

'Please do me a little favour,' he asked them. 'If you find that I have kept my promise and there are splendid new homes for you up there as I have described, then will you of your kindness fly up to the highest cave on the Hurricane Mountains and tell my sister Sootica that I am on my way to help her? Say that I have received her message and I am coming as fast as I can!'

The bats promised to do this.

So Gobbolino's disappointment was all the greater when the little wooden horse, standing on the belfry steps with the light of the early morning shining on the great new peace around them, said that he thought they ought to clean the church before they left.

CHAPTER 6

THE CHURCH IS SAVED

'IT will take us hours and hours!' said Gobbolino sadly.

The little wooden horse was already hunting in the vestry for dustpans and brushes, dusters and brooms. He sent Gobbolino outside to find a dustbin.

Gobbolino went out into the fresh morning air, very glad to be free of the bat-ridden church. He found a large dustbin, and also a tap with a pail underneath it, but he was in no mood for spring cleaning. He looked wistfully towards the Hurricane Mountains, envying the bats, who would be there by now, exploring the caves, and even making the acquaintance of his little sister Sootica.

There was one comfort – they would be telling her that he was coming.

He filled the bucket with water and carried it inside.

The little wooden horse had wasted no time in idleness. He was on the top of the belfry stairs sweeping the bell-ropes with the broom until no dirt or dust remained, and then he swept the bells. Beyond a faint chime every now and again no sound came out of them. They hung limp and heavy above the chancel far below. Gobbolino felt they must be very relieved to be at peace.

'Once the bats are gone and the church is really clean

again the people will come back!' said the little wooden horse, sweeping and polishing and mopping. Gobbolino joined in with a will, thinking the sooner the job was finished the better, and it was surprising how quickly they swept away the rubbish, washed the stones, and put the place to rights.

Shortly before midday the old priest returned, carrying a large plate of cold meat and a jug of milk. He nearly dropped these in his astonishment when he stepped inside the church. Gobbolino and the little wooden horse were just sweeping out the last of the dust and droppings, while the nave and the aisles gleamed with cleanliness. The pews shone.

'Oh my dear, good, kind little friends!' the old man said. 'How can I thank you enough? But I am afraid all your work will be in vain, because within a week the bats will have made it all dirty again, and nobody else has the courage to come and clean up after them.'

Gobbolino and the little wooden horse were so eager to explain that they both began to talk at once, and it was quite a while before they could make themselves understood.

'But do you mean to tell me . . .' the priest exclaimed, when at last he could make out their astonishing story, 'do you mean to say that the haunting which has terrified my whole parish was nothing more nor less than the bats jumping off the bell-ropes?'

'Just that!' said the little wooden horse and Gobbolino, nodding wisely.

'And that the bats are really gone for ever? So that

the church will stay clean and tidy and the bells will never clamour any more without a human hand to ring them?' the priest went on.

'The bats will never come back! They have gone to the caves on the Hurricane Mountains where there is room for thousands of bats!' Gobbolino said. 'So they will never ring the bells again, and your church will stay clean – that is if your parishioners are willing to keep it that way.'

'I can hardly believe it!' said the priest, his heart swelling with gratitude and happiness. 'So my prayers have been answered after all, and Good has banished Evil, just as I said. We must have a service of thanksgiving as soon as possible, and I will tell the congregation all about it. I must gather them all together! But first, we must ring the bells!'

Gobbolino and the little wooden horse stared at him in amazement, but the next moment each of them found himself at the end of a bell-rope. The old priest took a third, and directed them as he rang:

'One . . . two . . . three! One . . . two . . . three! One . . . two . . . three!'

The merry chimes rang out crystal clear, since the cleaning of the bronzes and scraping of the ropes had brought back the very best of their tones.

The notes were unmistakably clear and harmonious, and all round the parish where people had grown to dread the sound of the bells, they now stopped to listen.

'It is like the old days before the church was haunted!' the older ones said to each other. 'The priest is calling us to church. We had better go!'

One by one, or in twos and threes, even in family parties, they left their homes and walked to church, curious at the merry sound coming out of the church tower, a little apprehensive too, but trustful of their priest's bidding.

The priest begged Gobbolino and the little wooden horse to stay and take part in the service of thanksgiving. He wanted his parishioners to meet them, and to realize what had been done for them, once he had explained to them all that there was nothing more to fear. The bats who had been the cause of all the dread and terror were now many miles away in the mountains, and would never come back to the church.

Gobbolino and the little wooden horse were anxious to leave, for the day was far advanced, and they had many miles to go. It was all very well for the bats with their wings, they could fly leagues at a time without effort. But for wooden wheels, and paws unused to travelling, the distance was likely to be very exhausting.

There was also the faint risk that the hounds might return during the afternoon, and the sooner they took to the road the better.

However, the old priest was so insistent that they agreed to stay for a short while, and to slip out of the church before the sermon began. In this way they planned to avoid shaking hands and being introduced to all the congregation when the service was over. They felt they could not face a further delay in resuming their journey.

But now Gobbolino insisted that the little wooden horse should leave him to do the rest of the journey alone.

'Think how they are missing you at your home in the forest!' he reproached him. 'Uncle Peder is old, and so is his wife. Every evening they will be looking up the forest path and calling for you. You should have been sitting at home by the fire with them by now! I can see my destination ahead of me, and it cannot be very far away. Do go back, my kind little friend, and give me the pleasure of knowing that you are on your homeward journey!'

The little wooden horse was terribly reluctant to agree. He wanted to see Gobbolino safely across the plain to the foot of the mountains.

Yet all that he had said was true. The danger was over. There was not the smallest whisper of a hound's cry on the still afternoon air, while he knew how anxiously his dear old master would be looking for his return. The village was behind them, and they had travelled three parts of the plain. The little wooden horse had no fears that he would not be able to gallop back to the forest before darkness fell, and he would be home by early morning.

They stood looking at one another on a little hummock in the plain, one pleading for the other to go, the other pleading to stay.

'Just a little further!' begged the little wooden horse.

'Not one step, my kind friend!' said Gobbolino.

At last, very, very reluctantly, the little wooden horse agreed to say good-bye. He rubbed his wooden nose against Gobbolino's soft fur and asked him over and over again to come back as quickly as possible, and not to fail to call in at the cottage in the forest and relate all his adventures. Both of them knew that Gobbolino must cross the plain again on his homeward journey, and this time he would be all alone. Neither of them dared to think much about that.

For the second time the friends parted and proceeded in different directions. But this time the little wooden horse did not go far on his way. He crouched down in the grass to watch Gobbolino out of sight, quite determined to keep an eye upon him until he reached the mountains.

And so he saw what for a long time Gobbolino did not notice. A small black shadow was forming over the peaks, a shadow that circled and gyrated and gradually became bigger and bigger. For a while it looked like one of the small stormclouds that creep up into the sky on a summer's afternoon, and sometimes develop and sometimes come to nothing.

The little wooden horse took it for no more, no less than that. But as he watched his friend plodding purposefully onwards he realized that the cloud had left the peaks and was advancing to meet him. A summer thunderstorm would hurt nobody very seriously, however unpleasant it might be. But this cloud was different from a thunderstorm.

For one thing, there was no thunder. But there was a strange high noise of a kind one might meet in a tropical storm ... a high, screaming, whistling sound, almost beyond the normal range of an ear. And the cloud that had seemed so high now swooped lower and lower, till it was flying just above the level of the plain.

The bats were coming back!

CHAPTER 7

THE BATTLE OF THE BATS

THE awful realization struck the little wooden horse like a thunderclap. He stood up trembling on his little wooden legs.

It was not Gobbolino he was worrying about. It was not himself. What had brought the bats back out of the mountain caves he could not tell. Gobbolino had been responsible for their going there, but the agonizing thought in his own mind was the memory of the assembled congregation they had left behind them, all rejoicing in answer to their pastor's prayers, the sparkling clean church, the shining bells, and above all, the silence that he and Gobbolino had assured the priest would last for ever. Was it to be shattered so soon? Nobody would ever trust the priest's word again.

He hurried after Gobbolino, catching him just as the little cat stopped, and, raising himself on his hind legs, suddenly became aware of the advancing cloud of bats.

There were hundreds of them . . . no, not hundreds, but *thousands*! And they darkened the land beneath them as they flew southwards, uttering their shrill and indignant cries.

There was no doubt at all that they were angry.

At first it looked as if they would be passing to the right of the two friends, but at the last moment they caught sight of them, and the great cloud wheeled and dived on them, their cries even shriller as they screamed aloud:

'They're here! After them! Revenge! Revenge!'

The little wooden horse had arrived at Gobbolino's side. Both instinctively ducked their heads against the bats' attack, and the next minute they were in the centre of a whirling mass of raking claws, flashing teeth, and buffeting wings.

True enough, these made less impression on the wooden flanks of the little wooden horse than they did on Gobbolino, but on the other hand the cat was better

equipped to fight back with all four feet, and claws out-stretched. He too bit and scratched and hooked and tore, till the earth around him was strewn with wounded bats, but still they dived down row after row, and still Gobbolino bit and fought and the little wooden horse battered.

When there came the briefest pause in the fighting the little wooden horse jumped on to his hind legs and shouted at the top of his voice:

'Stop! Wait! Listen! Do us the honour, gentlemen, of telling us what we are fighting about! Why are you revenging yourselves on us, and what have we done to make you so angry?'

'Promises! Promises!' hissed the bats, stopping their attack for a moment. 'Empty promises! Deceit! Lies! False expectations! Empty, broken promises to get us out of our proper homes!'

'But didn't you find *better* homes in the caves?' asked Gobbolino in great surprise.

'Better, yes! Homes, no!' hissed the bats. 'Cave after cave we tried, and all in vain! No sooner had we found a home for our families than we were driven out again! Over and over and over again! There wasn't one cave in the whole of the mountains where we were allowed to stay and make a home!'

'But *who* drove you out? *Who* didn't let you stay?' asked Gobbolino.

'That wicked, ugly witch's cat!' chanted all the bats. 'The moment we were settled in, all nice and warm and comfortable, along she came and chased us out again! We complained to the witch, her mistress, but she only laughed! The selfishness of it!' shrieked the bats. 'Hundreds of empty caves! All perfect family homes for the asking, and no hope of getting even one for ourselves! You knew it when you sent us there! You did! You did! It was just a trick to get rid of us out of the church! And now we will have to go all the way back again, and nobody wants to have to sleep in the bell tower now we have seen those beautiful caves!'

But Gobbolino had no sympathy to spare for their troubles.

'What was the witch's cat like?' he asked eagerly. 'Did you notice her at all?'

'As if we could help it!' said the bats scornfully. 'She followed us everywhere! She was a fluffy black thing. She was rather like you!' they said rudely, pointing their wings at Gobbolino. 'Only her eyes were green, not blue, her fur was black, not tabby, and she had no white paw.'

'It *must* be my sister Sootica!' Gobbolino said to himself. 'Did you give her my message?' he asked the bats.

They were silent. At last one of them piped up:

'I'm sorry! I quite forgot!'

Gobbolino was bitterly disappointed.

'Tell me how she looked!' he pleaded. 'Was she sad? Or did she look happy? Did she seem ill-used, did you notice?'

'Happy? Sad? How could we tell?' said the bats. 'She was too busy chasing us to be sad or happy while we were there. She did say that her mistress the witch would beat her if she didn't get rid of us, because we interfered with her spells. All those beautiful caves! How could she need them all for her spells?'

The bats seemed to have lost their spirit for fighting. They began to close their ranks, ready to fly southwards again. The wounded ones picked themselves up and found they were not so badly hurt as they had imagined.

'Wait! Please wait!' Gobbolino begged them. 'You can't go back into the church until the people are gone, and they are all there saying their prayers and being thankful that the church is clean and tidy and not haunted any more.'

'Just let them wait till tonight!' jeered the bats. 'We'll give those bells such a clanging, we'll have everyone in the parish out of their beds with their hair standing on end!'

'Will you wait for just one more day?' pleaded the little wooden horse. 'My friend Gobbolino here received a message from his sister Sootica in the witch's cave. She said she needed his help, and asked him to come to her.'

'So you are a witch's cat too!' screamed the bats, preparing to fly at Gobbolino.

'Stop! Stop! Listen to me!' cried the little wooden horse. 'Gobbolino is *not* a witch's cat! He was badly used by the witch of the Hurricane Mountains, and she turned him into a common cat for ever and ever, but you can't blame a brother for going to the help of his sister. What would you do yourselves? What we do not know is *why* she needs him. And now it strikes me that we might well be able to bargain with Sootica for the caves, in return for whatever favour it is that she wants from Gobbolino. Wouldn't that be a better idea than going back to the church?'

The bats immediately became calmer, and agreed that this might be better than going back to the draughty belfry to sleep among the clanging bells.

'It means, of course, that you would have to come back with us to the mountains,' said the little wooden horse, 'and while we make our way up to the witch's cave you will have to arrange yourselves as best you can to pass the night in the rabbit burrows at the foot of the mountain. We shall do our best to arrange things to your best advantage, and you will have to play your part, as I have just said. I am sure it will all turn out for the best, for all of us.'

The faith and confidence of the little wooden horse put new heart into Gobbolino as well as the bats, who

agreed to go back to the mountains with the two friends.

'It is quite a long way,' they said, as they arranged their ranks. 'Wouldn't you prefer to ride with us?'

The little wooden horse and Gobbolino were only too glad to accept their offer, and watched with interest while a number of bats formed two circles by hooking themselves wing-tip to wing-tip, while others spread their wings within the circles and hooked themselves on to the sides. The result was a couple of flying hammocks, and in these Gobbolino and the little wooden horse deposited themselves very comfortably.

They flew off, leaving the plain far below them. Even the church tower was lost in the clouds, while the Hurricane Mountains loomed nearer and nearer.

Long ago Gobbolino had flown away from these same mountains behind his sister Sootica, on her broomstick, but on that occasion he had his back turned to the crags, and had not noticed how steep and savage they were. Now, the closer they approached the more fearsome they seemed, and he shivered at the thought of scaling them to find his sister and her mistress in the cavern. Sootica's message had been such a heartfelt cry, but her treatment of the bats was more like the normal practice of a witch's cat – it did not sound like the behaviour of a creature in distress. He became terribly worried, not only on his own account, but because he might be leading his friend, the little wooden horse, into danger.

The great cloud of bats wheeled round the base of the mountains, flying in circles lower and lower, until it deposited them both on the grass. There were sandy banks here, and these were riddled with rabbits' burrows.

The bats were rather dissatisfied with these, but they agreed to spend one night only in the holes, while Gobbolino and the little wooden horse did what they could to get possession of the caves for them.

The little wooden horse refused to go home until this was done. He had a growing feeling that Gobbolino would need all the help he could find in the next part of his adventure, and he did not mean to abandon his friend until it seemed quite safe to do so.

CHAPTER 8

SOOTICA

LEAVING the bats to find shelter for themselves in the rabbit holes, Gobbolino and the little wooden horse began to climb the very steep and narrow path between the rocks to the summit of the mountain.

Now that he was back again in this bleak and unfriendly country Gobbolino became very nervous, and said no more about sending the little wooden horse home. If his friend had left him Gobbolino would hardly have had the courage to climb on alone, so dark and angry were the crags, and so steep the track below them. The sun was rapidly leaving the sky, and the rocks were cold and blue.

For a short while they could still hear the squeaking of the bats below, but soon these sounds died away and they were terribly alone.

The path wound up and up and up. The sun went down, and the mountains seemed to be covered in a great black counterpane. The moon had not yet risen, and the stars were very faint. It was not a good place to be caught in at night, but neither of them wanted to arrive after dark in the witch's cavern.

Round a corner they came upon one of the many caves squeezed in between the rocks – caves that the bats had not been allowed to claim for their own. The cave was empty now, and the friends looked at one another with one single thought in their minds. If they crept inside and spent the night in the cave they might face the next morning with more courage, and in daylight. They did not need to say a word aloud to each other, but turning off the path they stole inside.

Gobbolino felt much safer when the walls of the cave were around him, and he was deadly tired. He lay down close beside the body of the little wooden horse, and almost immediately fell asleep.

The little wooden horse stayed awake only long enough to make sure that the cave was quite empty, and that no strange noises threatened them from the mountain above. His wooden heart beat pit-a-pat, pit-a-pat, for he did not like this part of the country any better than Gobbolino did. But nothing would have persuaded him to desert his friend, although he could not help thinking very anxiously about his dear master back there in the forest, who would be daily expecting him to come home.

Their adventure had scarcely begun, since they did not know why Gobbolino's sister had sent such a piteous message, nor what kind of trouble she might be in.

'But there is nothing I can do about it till the morning,' said the little wooden horse very sensibly, so he too went off to sleep.

When he woke up the cave was full of moonlight. It shone straight in from the entrance, and standing in the middle of it, looking straight at him, was Gobbolino.

The little wooden horse leapt to his feet. He thought Gobbolino must be leaving without him, taking advan-

tage of the moonlight and not wanting to waste any more time waiting in the cave.

But Gobbolino was coming *into* the cave, not going out, and his face did not wear the kind and friendly expression that the little wooden horse had learnt to know so well. It wore a suspicious, rather fierce look, and he now noticed that the cat's eyes were flashing with a green light, not blue, and that all its paws were black. It was so exactly like Gobbolino in every other way that the little wooden horse had to stare at it again and again to make sure he had not made a mistake, and this *was* his friend after all.

But if he had any doubts left these were quickly dispelled by a flurry of dark fur at his side. Three black paws and one white one sprang out of the shadows in a single bound, as Gobbolino's voice cried joyfully:

'Sister! My sister Sootica! Is it really you? Oh, sister! sister! How glad I am to see you!'

The two cats fell upon each other, licking and purring.

The green fire died down in Sootica's eyes. She seemed overwhelmed with joy to see her brother. The cave resounded with their joyous miaows and purrs, and the little wooden horse was feeling slightly left out in the cold when suddenly Gobbolino remembered him, and proudly introduced him to his sister.

'My best, my most true and trusted friend!' he said. 'I would not be here at all if it had not been for him!'

'Well I never! Well I never!' said Sootica, walking round and round the little wooden horse. It was quite evident that she had not seen anything like him before.

'Where do you come from?' she asked curiously. 'And what are you doing here?'

'I came to help my friend Gobbolino in answering your plea,' said the little wooden horse solemnly. He could not help noticing that Sootica looked perfectly healthy and able to look after herself. She did not appear harassed, or in distress, nor, in fact, in any kind of trouble at all.

'The owl brought me the message that you sent, sister!' said Gobbolino eagerly. 'I started out that very same morning, and here I am! And why did you send for me, sister? Please tell me why!'

The eyes of the witch's cat half closed, and grew cunning.

'I was missing you, brother,' she whined, looking at him through green slits, 'I was feeling so lonesome without you! But I thought you would come by yourself! I did not expect you to bring a friend!'

Sootica did not seem at all at ease with the little wooden horse. Every time she looked at him she shifted from one black paw to another, and she kept walking round and round him, staring.

'You needn't be nervous, sister,' said Gobbolino, 'he is the best and bravest little horse in all the world! And if we can do anything between us to help you, let us know quickly what it is, because in the forest Uncle Peder will be anxiously waiting for his horse to come home, and I promised the children at the farm that I would not be long away.'

Suddenly the witch's cat lost all her bravado. Her green eyes filled with tears, and she looked piteously at the two friends.

'I want to be a kitchen cat too!' she sobbed. 'I am tired of being a witch's cat! My mistress gets more and more bad-tempered every day! I am never allowed to do as I please. I have to work at making spells and practising wickednesses from dawn till dark! I don't enjoy it any more! I want a safe and happy home like yours to live in!'

Gobbolino was very distressed. He knew how he had suffered himself while trying to find a home when he was half a witch's cat, and here was his sister Sootica, steeped in spells and sin, but longing to settle down in some safe and happy home while she was still under the power of a witch. How could she imagine such a thing was possible? And how long would she be satisfied to live the life of a common mouser? How far could she be trusted to behave like an ordinary cat, and not get up to tricks which, as Gobbolino knew, were sure to be worse and more unpleasant than any he had ever learnt himself. And how likely was it that the witch would allow her to go free? A witch relies on her cat to stay by her side for ever and ever. She would not part with Sootica just for the asking.

'How can you bear to give up the life you told me was so exciting?' Gobbolino reproached her.

'I am tired of my exciting life, brother!' said Sootica simply, and the tears rolled out of her green eyes down to the black fur of her bib. 'I want to be good and happy like you!'

'For ever?' said Gobbolino, disbelievingly.

'For ever!' Sootica repeated, nodding vigorously.

'Your mistress threw me into her cauldron to turn me into a kitchen cat,' said Gobbolino. 'When I came out I wasn't a witch's cat any longer. Would she do the same for you?'

'Oh no! . . . never, never, never!' shuddered Sootica. 'I wouldn't tell her I was leaving her, because if I did she would never let me out of the cave again! I must come with you secretly, while she is asleep. In the early morning, perhaps, when she is fast asleep after being out all night, and she won't notice if I am there or not.'

'But if she were to wake up and find you gone,' shuddered Gobbolino, 'she would be sure to chase you, and she would catch us all three!'

'Oh she would! She would!' chuckled Sootica, her tears drying. 'But I have a trick worth two of that! We must pass through running water! Witches can't pass through running water, or even over it, but witches' cats can! We'll be quite safe when we have done that!'

Gobbolino thought of the stream halfway across the plain, where they had eaten their dinner. He thought too of the hounds that had chased them, and suddenly remembered the bats.

'If you were to come back with us, would the bats be able to live in the caves at the foot of these mountains?' he asked his sister. 'Because we promised them we would try to arrange it, and they would not have to go back to the church belfry and disturb the villagers any more.'

'Oh the bats!' said Sootica scornfully. 'They can sleep anywhere they please for all I care! My mistress will soon get tired of turning them out of the caves when she hasn't got me to do it for her!'

The little wooden horse had not said anything for a long while, but now he spoke, looking very gravely at the witch's cat, Sootica.

'I think you are intending to behave very badly towards your mistress,' he said severely. 'After all, hasn't she brought you up since you were a kitten? Hasn't she fed you, and given you a home, and taught you all you know? Bad she may be, but she is your mistress and you owe it to her to be faithful. What is she going to do for a cat if you leave her like this?'

'I'm sure I don't know, and I certainly don't care!' said Sootica crossly.

'Do go and ask her permission first, sister,' urged Gobbolino. 'Perhaps she will allow you to leave if you really want it so badly!'

'You are perfectly crazy if you think so, brother,' said Sootica scornfully. 'Do you really think that at her age she wants to train up another kitten to be as clever as me? Not likely!'

'Just as I told you!' retorted the little wooden horse. 'You really cannot be so inconsiderate towards your mistress. Make the best of the life you have chosen, my friend – I can assure you that you would soon get tired of living the quiet existence of a kitchen cat, like your brother Gobbolino!'

'I would never get tired of it!' scowled Sootica.

'Perhaps your mistress still has the spell in the cauldron that she dipped me in!' said Gobbolino suddenly. 'And if she has, you have only to dip yourself in it and all will be settled in an instant. Once you are an ordinary cat the witch will not want to have you, and you will never want to be a witch's cat again!'

'Ha!' laughed Sootica scornfully. 'You do have some foolish ideas in your head, my poor silly brother! Why, when I returned from dropping you off the back of my broomstick on to your happy farmyard home, the witch had already tipped the rest of the spell down the mountainside! No, there is no hope for it but to escape, and I intend to come with you first thing in the morning!'

'But why did you send for me if you meant to escape in any case?' asked Gobbolino, puzzled.

At once the eyes of the witch's cat became sly, and she half closed them again.

'I will tell you how you can help me, brother!' she said. 'My mistress is old and getting very blind. She would never know the difference between us if, for a few hours, you took my place, just long enough for me to reach the plain and across the water that will break her power over me. Only a very few hours, Gobbolino! Just long enough for you to hide your tabby coat in the shadows while she sleeps away the daylight, and as long as she thinks it is me sleeping in the corner she will not take the slightest notice of you. Do just this little favour for me, brother, and I will be grateful to you for the rest of my life.'

Gobbolino's ears flattened on his head from sheer terror at such a dreadful idea.

'But my paw! My white paw! And my eyes are blue!' he protested helplessly.

'You must keep your eyes half closed and she will

71

never notice the colour!' cried Sootica. 'And I shall
black your paw with dirt off the walls. After all, it is
only for such a little while!' she coaxed him. 'My mistress
sleeps for hours and hours after her night excursions,
and I can assure you you will be as safe up there in her
cave as by your own fireside at home!'

'Oh no! no! no!' sobbed Gobbolino, while the little
wooden horse stood up as straight as a wooden soldier
beside him, determined to defend his friend to the last.

'You ought to be ashamed of yourself, Mistress Sootica!' he exclaimed. 'How can you ask such a thing of
your brother? It is wicked and cruel and heartless, and if
I have any say in the matter he shall do no such thing!'

'And I shall have to stay a witch's cat for ever and
ever!' said Sootica subsiding into tears. 'Very well! You
are selfish and cold-hearted, the pair of you! And it is
you who ought to be ashamed of yourselves! There you
are both of you with happy homes, and a welcome waiting for each of you when you return; but here am I,
doomed to a miserable existence for the rest of my life. I
hope you will think of me now and again when you are
warm and purring by your own hearth, brother! We
were born and bred side by side, but look at us now!'

Gobbolino was nearly sobbing himself.

It all came back to him, the wretched hours and days
and weeks he had spent in the witch's cave, a slave to
her powers and her spells and her mischief. He had
never been so miserable in all his life as in those days,
and now he was going to abandon his sister to the same
fate, rather than help her, just for the shortest possible
time, to make her escape.

He looked at the little wooden horse.

'It would be very much better not to do as she asks,' said the horse. 'I think you will regret it if you do!'

'I only want to be good like you are!' wept Sootica. 'I don't want to be wicked any more! Won't you help me to be good, dear friends? Or are you going to abandon me for ever and ever and ever?'

Even the little wooden horse was silent now.

It was a problem bigger than any he had had to deal with. On the one hand, there was the well-being and safety of his friend Gobbolino, and on the other the saving of a fellow creature, steeped to be sure in wickedness, but who might, if they helped her, turn into something better.

The one person he could think of who might make a good cat of Sootica for the rest of her nine lives was his dear old Uncle Peder. But the risk! Oh the awful risk of such an undertaking, even for a few short hours!

While they all stood dumbly facing one another in the moonlight a shrill and far-off screeching summoned Sootica from the top of the mountain. It was the witch, calling for her cat to join her on her night's excursions.

Sootica shot to her feet with her fur standing on end.

'My mistress! I must go before she sees you!' she exclaimed. 'Brother! I beseech you to do this one thing for me! Just this one little thing! Meet me high up on the mountain when the sun touches the topmost crag, and I will show you where to hide yourself! Please brother! Oh do! Oh do! Just think! You will be giving me my last chance of happiness!'

There came another screech from above, and Sootica shot out of the cave and was gone.

CHAPTER 9

SOOTICA'S PLAN

GOBBOLINO and the little wooden horse stood looking at each other in great perplexity and even despair. Their legs felt weak with terror at Sootica's suggestion, and even the little wooden horse could think of nothing positive to say.

'If we left her now,' Gobbolino said at last, 'we could be back in the forest before dark! But what would become of my poor sister? And then there are the bats! We have promised to help them. How can we be so selfish as to abandon them now, to help ourselves? If they can't use the caves they will fly back to the village and harass the priest and the congregation. Surely we can't allow that to happen?'

The little wooden horse could only shake his head very sorrowfully. The whole plan filled him with dread and foreboding.

He did not doubt that Sootica really did long to leave the witch and become an ordinary cat, like her brother, but even if her escape was successful and they all arrived safely home, would she really make a kitchen cat after her long training in a witch's cave? And even more important than that, what awful risks did his friend Gobbolino run in taking her place? What would the witch do if she caught him at it? He began to shiver in all his little wooden legs.

But Gobbolino was making plans, and the more positive the plans the braver he felt about coming to a decision.

'You and Sootica must start for home the moment the sun rises over the top of the mountain,' he announced. 'In that way you can be at the river by midday, avoiding the village. Then, if the witch is still asleep as my sister supposes, I will leave the cave and follow you. Once we are across the water we shall all be safe.'

'I shall not go with your sister Sootica,' said the little wooden horse with outraged dignity. 'I shall wait and come with you!'

'Oh no!' said Gobbolino. 'Because my sister will not be safe until she has crossed the stream, and while she is still this side of the bank the witch can still catch her, if by any unlucky chance she finds out the trick we are playing on her. You must go with her, and swim her across on your back as you did me.'

'But she can swim herself! Witches' cats can swim!' protested the little wooden horse. 'Witches may not be able to cross spring water, but their cats can! And I'm not going from here while you are still in danger!'

At the word 'danger' Gobbolino shivered again, but he tried to disguise his fears.

'You must think of your dear old friends waiting for you!' he told the little wooden horse. 'If anything happens to me you can explain it when you come to Uncle Peder and his wife, and they will tell the farmer and his family. Why, they may even take in my sister Sootica for my sake!'

But the little wooden horse would not hear of leaving the Hurricane Mountains without Gobbolino.

'We will think about it in the morning,' he said, still very troubled, and side by side they lay down to sleep until dawn.

They slept so long and so late after their adventures of the day before that they forgot to wake up in time to climb the peak and meet Sootica on her return from her excursion with the witch. In fact, daylight was streaming into the cave, and the little wooden horse was just congratulating himself that it was now too late to carry out Sootica's horrid plan, when the cat herself tore into the cave, bursting with indignation.

'Ah! So you are still here!' she cried in triumph. 'I thought you must be gone! Coward and humbug!' she spat at Gobbolino. 'You said you had come to save me, and already you have left me to my fate!'

'Oh no, sister! Oh no! Indeed I have not!' cried Gobbolino, springing up and rubbing the sleep out of his beautiful blue eyes. 'I am ready! I am ready!'

'Stop!' cried the little wooden horse, but Sootica pushed past him and collected some black mould from the rocks at the side of the cave.

'Give me your paw, brother!' she commanded, and in a minute or two Gobbolino's paws were all as black as one another.

'Keep your eyes half shut,' she told him. 'Look out through the slits as I do! My mistress has been asleep for half an hour already, the morning is well on its way. We have no time to lose. Follow me!'

The little wooden horse protested in vain. Gobbolino ran out of the cave after his sister Sootica, and together they galloped up the steep mountain path to the crest. The little wooden horse was not far behind them. But they had not gone far before the witch's cat rounded on him:

'Go back! Go back!' she hissed. 'Your wooden wheels make such a noise my mistress will wake up and hear you coming! You must stay a long way behind us, or else not come at all!'

Very crestfallen the little wooden horse fell back, turning his wooden wheels very carefully so as to make no noise at all. His heart ached unbearably to see his friend Gobbolino disappearing round a corner of the

path far above his head, just one pace behind his sister
Sootica. He dared not hurry, for fear of waking the
witch, and it seemed to him that the two little cats had
been gone for hours on end when suddenly Sootica
appeared, coming towards him on the path just above
his head.

She passed him like a streak of summer lightning, her
eyes shining with green fire.

'I'm off!' she cried with a wild laugh of triumph. 'And
my brother has taken my place . . . all curled up by the

side of my mistress the witch! I'll meet you both on the far side of the stream, after midday! Don't venture any higher up, my friend, if you value your life. If my mistress catches sight of you there's no saying what she may do to the pair of you! At midday, with luck, my brother will join you in the cave below, and you can both follow me to the river! Be careful! Be very careful! Good-bye! Good-bye!'

She was gone, and the little wooden horse was left alone on the mountain path, terrified by the thought of what might happen to Gobbolino if either of them were seen by the witch.

He decided to do as Sootica suggested, and wait in the cave below until midday. It was not so long, after all, and yet it seemed a thousand years ahead.

CHAPTER 10

IN THE WITCH'S CAVE

IF it seemed a long time to the little wooden horse it seemed ten times as long to Gobbolino, curled up in a dark corner of the witch's cave beside the ugly old woman whose face he remembered so well. He shrank into the shadows among the cobwebs and dust, hoping she would not notice him if she woke up. Sootica had assured him that she would sleep till sunset, but his heart beat so loudly he was afraid it might rouse her, and the harder he tried to suppress it the louder it beat.

There next to her was the same cauldron he had been forced to stir, and beside which he had fallen asleep in the middle of making the witch's most important spell. He wondered what the cauldron contained today.

There too were the spiders, and one or two lazy bats, hanging in the rocks above the cauldron. It was all so familiar he began to feel he had never left it, and yet how different it all was from his happy farmyard home!

He tried to imagine his sister Sootica at the farm, but he could not. It was much more natural to think of her in this shadowy cave beside the snoring witch. Gobbolino tried not to look at the witch, but her snoring made him very nervous, especially when it stopped for a little and then went on again.

He pictured Sootica tearing down the mountainside,

past the little wooden horse, who he hoped was now starting for home, but he knew his loyal little friend was more likely to be waiting for him in the cave below.

He hoped Sootica would remember to stop and tell the bats that by evening their caves would be free for them And suddenly he remembered how the bats had carried them to the mountain. Perhaps they would help them again! In gratitude for the caves they might even carry them back to the river! This thought was so hopeful and comforting that his heart actually settled down and began to beat less noisily, but that only made the witch's snores the louder.

Through the open doorway he could see the sun painting the crags with gold.

'When it reaches *that* one . . .' Sootica had told him, pointing with her paw, 'it will be midday, and I shall be safely across the river, so you can leave the cave and come after me. You will have arrived there yourself by the time my mistress wakes up, so you have nothing to fear!'

The long morning crawled by. Outside, Gobbolino could see that the view from the mountain top was very beautiful. The sun warmed the rocks below and beyond, slowly spreading a flush of colour higher and higher like the sweep of a gigantic paintbrush. Yet it moved so slowly Gobbolino wondered if it would ever reach the rock Sootica had pointed out to him, and allow him to go free.

What would happen, he asked himself, if he left the cave early, before the sun reached midday?

For one thing, the witch could easily awake early

herself, and find her cat gone. Searching and calling, she might fly down the mountainside and overtake him, or she might soar very high into the sky on her broomstick and see, not only himself, but Sootica making her way to the river across the plain. And when she had pounced down on her cat, and brought her back to the cave the bats would be forbidden the caves below, and things would be just as bad as they had been before. What his own punishment would be Gobbolino did not dare to think. At the moment he was more concerned about Sootica and the bats.

One thing consoled him. The witch had nothing against the little wooden horse. She did not even know he was there, and provided he kept himself out of her sight he was quite safe, whether plodding home across the plain, or hiding in the cave where they had passed

the night. Gobbolino preferred to think that he was on his way back to the forest, and that by nightfall they might be there together.

The bats and the spiders in the witch's cave took no notice of him, and a wrinkled old toad in the corner merely stared at him for a while and then shut its eyes again and went back to sleep.

Gobbolino was very thirsty. He was hungry too, for he had not eaten since the tasty dinner brought to them in the church by the old priest the day before, but he dared not touch the strange-looking food in the witch's cooking pan, nor take a drink from the cauldron, for fear of the magic it might hold. Presently, above the snores of the witch, he noticed the steady drip of water not far from him, and saw a tiny spring far above his head, that spattered a drop or so of crystal clear water onto the stones at every minute.

Very thankfully and carefully Gobbolino moved towards it and held out a grateful tongue to the drops of
water. They tasted very cold and sweet. Some of the
water had formed a tiny pool in the hollow of a rock,
and this he drank too, but very quietly, in case the witch
should hear his lapping.

He felt better now, and told himself that at least three
hours must have passed since Sootica went away, for the
sun had moved quite a distance across the rocks.

Presently he noticed that the witch's snoring had
changed a little. It was no longer so loud and regular as
it had been in the early morning, when it had been
rather like listening to a clock ticking. Even the short
pauses that had frightened him so much had become
part of a rhythm that seemed set to go on for ever. But
now the snoring became lighter, and rather quicker, as
if the witch were dreaming . . . as if her dreams were
disturbing her . . . as if they were waking her up . . .

She gave a little shriek . . . a cough . . . a hiccup . . .
and then the snoring stopped altogether.

Gobbolino froze with terror. He was in the darkest,
most shadowy corner of the cave, but who could tell
how much witches were able to see in the dark?

He listened, hoping that she would settle down and
begin to snore again, but meanwhile she was moving,
and clearing her throat . . . yes, and muttering . . . the
witch was awake!

Silence fell. Gobbolino could hear her shuffling her
feet, and then – horror of horrors! – she was getting up!

He shut his eyes as tightly as possible, so that the gleam in them should not catch her attention, and heard her shuffling across the floor to the doorway.

She stood there for a while, looking out at the morning, but it seemed that the sunshine was not to her liking, for she came back grumbling, and began to move round the cavern looking for her stick.

'Sootica!' she muttered, and then louder, 'Sootica! Puss! Puss! Where are you? I'm calling you, Sootica!'

Gobbolino froze.

Perhaps if he did not move she would think her cat had gone outside on to the mountain. She might even fall asleep again, waiting for Sootica to come back.

But the witch did not seem inclined to settle down and go to sleep. She walked round and round the cave grumbling and calling for her cat in a louder and louder voice till Gobbolino cringed with fear. Once she passed so close to him that she scuffed him with her shoe, but she did not know what she had touched.

Gobbolino remembered that his sister had told him that her mistress was getting rather blind.

At last she found her stick, and now the search for Sootica began in earnest, as if the witch knew by instinct that her cat was not far away. The stick went tap tap tap across the floor as she poked and prodded in the corners, and in the holes behind the rocks. Now and then she went to the doorway and yelled Sootica's name in louder and louder tones, but she always came back into the cave, looking very puzzled and dissatisfied.

Suddenly, as she passed him for the third time, Gobbolino received a painful poke in the ribs from the stick, and at once the witch stopped short.

She poked again, and Gobbolino was forced to move away to avoid the painful prods that seemed likely to crack his ribs if he did not escape from them.

'So there you are!' cried the witch in triumph, hitting out with her stick where she thought he might be. Gobbolino shot out of his corner and took refuge behind the cauldron.

'Lazy, good-for-nothing creature!' cried the witch, slashing at the rocks. 'Why didn't you answer when I called you? Afraid I was going to set you to work, were you? Where are you? Come out and show yourself, wherever you are!'

Gobbolino thought it best to obey her, while keeping well out of the way of her stick.

She saw him now, and flung a little clay pot in his direction.

'Go and fetch me some honey, now that you have taken the trouble to show yourself!' she ordered him. 'I'm hungry, and I want something sweet. You know where the bees' nest is. Round the corner between the rocks! Go quickly!'

Gobbolino did as he was told. He snatched up the pot and ran from the cave, glad to be out of her reach, though not at all sure where to find the honey.

Fortunately the bees were busying to and fro, and he had only to watch them to find the hole between the rocks where they had their honeycombs. He could even see the sticky golden honey gleaming inside the cleft, and closing his eyes he bravely plunged his paw inside and filled the pot.

Where a true witch's cat would have escaped without harm, the bees were quick to set about a mere kitchen cat raiding their store, and Gobbolino had several painful stings on his paw before the pot was full. He was forced to stop and lick it to ease the pain, and it was not until he had given the whole foot a long and comforting wash that he saw to his horror he had licked off the black covering his sister had painted on to hide his white markings.

He did not know what to do, and meanwhile the witch was bellowing at him from the cave, so carrying the pot carefully in his other paw he limped along to serve her.

'That's better!' the witch said, smacking her lips over the honey 'Now I shall have another little doze. But first you can go and get me a drink of milk from the wild goats. They are just over the crest there. I can hear them. And the pipkin is hanging by the door.'

Gobbolino was only too glad to escape out of her sight. He snatched the milk jug and limped across the rocks to find the goats, who, when they looked up and saw him, knew in a moment that he was not Sootica, and proceeded to tease him and lead him a merry dance from crag to crag.

'Oh please! Oh please!' he begged them. 'Just a little drop of milk! Not much! Please stop just for one moment and let me fill my little jug! The witch will kill me if you don't!' sobbed Gobbolino, quite out of breath and at the end of his endurance.

At last one of the goats felt sorry for him and stopped her cavorting.

'Why, you don't even know how to milk a goat, my poor cat!' it said pityingly. 'Don't they teach you common cats anything at all?'

Gobbolino was ashamed to explain that his paws were swollen with stings from the bees. He did the best he could, and the goat was patient.

Presently the jug was full, but not fast enough to please the witch, who was standing at the mouth of the cave, shrieking at him when at last he arrived with the milk.

'Dawdling and gossiping!' she scolded. 'The goats are the worst gossips in the world, next to *you*, lazy, good-for-nothing cat! Fetch me a cup and pour me out a drink! You can keep a drop for yourself, but only a drop, mind!'

She followed Gobbolino back into the cave, where he spent a little time in finding a cup, and took the opportunity of rubbing a fresh coating of dirt over his paw. He was rewarded by a prod in the ribs and a fresh burst of scolding.

Fortunately he was able to pour out the milk with his back turned towards the witch, and he passed it to her with his left paw. He was very grateful to have a good drink himself, and the goat's milk tasted very good and wholesome. He was just returning to his own corner when the witch called him out again.

'Feel the water in the cauldron, Sootica! Feel if it is getting hot! I want it ready and boiling by nightfall!'

Gobbolino put a paw nervously on the side of the

cauldron, expecting to be burned, but it was only luke-warm.

'Not like that, you lazy cat! Get up on your hind legs and feel the water inside it!' the witch cried sharply, and she came to stand over him while he dipped his right paw into the liquid, where the oily bubbles swam round and round at his stirring.

'Not that paw! Will you never remember what I have taught you?' screeched the witch. 'You must always stir a spell with your left paw, or you may spoil it before you begin! Go on then! Tell me if it is getting hot!'

Gobbolino was forced to obey her, and almost im-mediately the dirt was washed off his paw, which gleamed pure white in the murky cave before he could hide it out of sight.

The witch stared at it, and gave a gasp of horror. Then she seized Gobbolino by the neck and held him up in front of her, staring into his face.

'Sootica! *Sootica!*' she cried aloud. 'Why, you wretched little impostor, you are not my cat at all!'

'No, ma'am! I'm sorry, ma'am!' gasped Gobbolino, his eyes wide with fright. 'But I'll do my best to serve you, ma'am! I assure you I will!'

He expected at any moment to be thrown into the cauldron, or else taken to the entrance of the cavern and hurled down the Hurricane Mountains as the witch had threatened to do long ago, but for the moment she dropped him on the ground and stared at him very thoughtfully.

'White paw! . . . blue eyes!' she muttered. 'Why, I do believe . . . I do declare I have seen you before! I believe

you are brother to my own good-for-nothing cat! And
once, long ago, you were both here together in my
cavern. Am I right, cat?'

'Yes, ma'am! If you please, ma'am!' said Gobbolino,
lowering his beautiful blue eyes to the floor.

'*Then what are you doing here now?*' thundered the witch
in a terrible voice.

Gobbolino could think of nothing better to say than:
'I beg your pardon, ma'am!'

'And where is my cat Sootica?' demanded the witch.

Gobbolino was in a terrible quandary. He did not know how far on her journey his sister might have travelled, but he was almost certain the witch would be after her in a minute if he confessed their plans. What he did not know was that witches can see very little by day, and are afraid of sunlight. It was most unlikely that she would chase after Sootica until nightfall.

He went on looking at the floor and said nothing.

'Do you mean to tell me you have not seen her at all?' asked the witch.

'Oh yes, ma'am, I saw her!' confessed Gobbolino.

'WHERE did you see her?' demanded the witch.

'Why, in the cave, ma'am, all in the moonlight,' said Gobbolino.

'But this morning . . . when the sun rose . . .?'

'When I woke up in the morning she was gone,' said Gobbolino truthfully.

'I see it all! I see it all!' raged the witch. 'She has left me! My cat has deserted me! And she put you in her place to deceive me while she escaped! Isn't that true, kitchen cat?'

'Yes, ma'am!' said Gobbolino, trembling and expecting to be destroyed at any minute.

But the witch sat down on her stool and rocked herself to and fro.

'Why did she leave me . . . oh why?' she moaned, with grey tears pouring down her shrivelled cheeks. 'All these months I fed and trained her, and taught her all she knows. She had become the best witch's cat in all the world! Why should she want to leave me here alone now that I am old and getting helpless? She knows I can't get on without her! She knows I can't even make a spell without her to read it to me out of my book. How could she desert me? How could she be so cruel? Has she gone to find a younger witch, who can teach her more than I can? So selfish! So unkind! If I had anything more to show her I would have taught it to her . . . she knows that! I'm so old! I can't go on for ever! Witches depend on their cats to stay beside them till they die! Didn't she know it would kill me to let her go?'

The more the witch sobbed and cried the less like a

witch she appeared and the more like a lonely old woman.

'Wasn't I wicked enough for her?' she moaned, till Gobbolino's heart was touched, and he cautiously rubbed his body against her legs.

'I think my sister had got tired of being a witch's cat,' he told her. 'I think she wanted to be a good cat for a change.'

'*Good?*' said the witch, quite startled. 'How could she be good? She was born and bred a witch's cat!'

Gobbolino said nothing, and the witch's eye fell on him again. 'Oh *you*!' she said scornfully. 'You were only born half a witch's kitten! Look at your white paw and your blue eyes! Poor miserable little creature, when I changed you back into a kitchen cat I had only to finish off what was already begun. But my beautiful black Sootica! How could she treat me so badly? How could she break my old heart? She has left me. And where is she now?'

The old witch went back to sobbing and crying and rocking herself to and fro, till Gobbolino did not know how to comfort her. She seemed to have lost all her desire to punish him, in fact one of her claw-like hands was actually caressing and rubbing his neck as if he were Sootica his sister. The feel of his fur seemed to comfort her a little.

'What shall I do? What shall I do?' she sobbed over and over again, and Gobbolino was so overcome with pity that he crept on to her lap, and lay down as close to her crabby old heart as he could push himself.

But her tears and sobs went on and on. He had never

known anyone cry so long or so bitterly. He found himself blaming his sister Sootica for her selfishness and her desertion. If he had known how her escape would affect the old witch he would never have agreed to help her. Danger was one thing, desertion was another, and here was a poor old woman in the throes of bitter despair. Gobbolino was bitterly ashamed of his sister, and wondered how in the world he could fetch her back.

The old woman slowly sobbed herself off to sleep, but Gobbolino would not creep from her lap for fear of waking her to a new sense of loss. He was willing to give her what little comfort he could.

Meanwhile the sun crept slowly up the rocks and touched the crag that signified midday.

Gobbolino watched it.

Now Sootica would have reached the river! Now she would have swum across it and the witch could no longer capture her and bring her home. Half of Gobbolino rejoiced at her escape. The other half reproached her for her selfishness and cruelty in leaving her old mistress. Could she really hope to become a good kitchen cat if she began with such behaviour?

He shifted his paws, and the witch gave a little sobbing moan.

'Puss! Pretty Pusskins!' she murmured, but Gobbolino knew she was mistaking him for his sister.

Slowly the sun crossed the sky and moved across the rocks. He had a long way to go before nightfall, but if he left now he might just cross the plain before it became too dark to see his way. His friend, the little wooden horse, would be waiting for him in the shade of the

94

forest, and oh! the joy of having his companionship again! He felt comforted by the very thought.

His fur was damp with the witch's tears. He could not find it in his heart to leave her just yet. Perhaps, a little later, when she woke up, and seemed a little less wretched, he would go down the path and maybe spend the night in one of the caves with the bats below. He did not think the witch would want to harm him now. And she could not have any real interest in a common kitchen cat.

He dozed off on her skinny lap, and slept for a couple of hours.

When he awoke the cave entrance was golden with afternoon sunshine, and he thought he heard someone coming up the hill. It must be Sootica!

But the person who suddenly appeared in the cavern entrance was not Sootica, but the little wooden horse!

CHAPTER 11

AT THE FOOT OF THE MOUNTAIN

THE little wooden horse had waited patiently hour after hour for his friend to reappear.

Like Gobbolino, he had watched the sun moving across the sky, and he knew that by midday Sootica was likely to have reached the river, and would therefore be safe from recapture by the witch.

He did not approve of her behaviour in the least, but he could understand the tender heart of a brother for his sister's distress, if, in fact, the witch's cat were really as distressed as she made herself out to be.

He saw the sun touch the midday crag, and pass on slowly across the jagged peaks of the mountain. At any moment he expected to see Gobbolino come flying down the mountainside, but Gobbolino did not come.

After an hour or two the little horse began to grow anxious. He did not want to be stranded in the middle of the plain when the sun went down. There was no shelter out there, while in the forest they could pass the night under a tree.

He trotted out of the cave and looked up towards the summit, but there was nothing to be seen of Gobbolino.

He waited while another hour crawled by, and then began very slowly to descend towards the bats, who were restlessly flying about below, and waiting to take possession of the caves at the foot of the mountain. They were in a very testy frame of mind, due to sleeping in rabbit holes and having nothing much to eat.

They took very little notice of the wooden horse, flying around in crazy circles and alighting on the rocks, only to dash around again like a crowd of mad mosquitoes. Not one of them volunteered to go up to the top of the mountain and remind Gobbolino that it was high time he started down the path to begin his journey home across the plain. They were afraid of being caught by the witch, and either having to stay in the cavern under her command, or being banished back to the rabbit holes again. Finally he persuaded a very young and dashing bat to go up the mountain.

'Just tell my friend Gobbolino that we should leave immediately,' the little wooden horse said, 'that is, if we want to travel safely across the plain before dark. Tell him I am waiting for him down here, and I shall not set out until he comes.'

The bat whirred off in the direction of the summit. The wooden horse waited impatiently below.

It was some while before the bat came back, appearing like a small black fly against the sky above, soon to be lost in the darkness of the crags. The little wooden horse lost sight of it in craning for a glimpse of Gobbolino, but the path remained empty, and there was no sign of his friend.

Suddenly the bat flopped down at his feet, panting.

'I waited and waited,' it squeaked, 'but it was no good – he won't come!'

'He won't come?' the little wooden horse repeated in

dismay. 'Is the witch awake, then? Has she put a spell on him?'

'Not that I could notice,' said the little bat. 'I think the witch is asleep, because she is snoring a little . . . and your friend Gobbolino is fast asleep too, on her lap.'

'On her lap?' the little wooden horse cried out, in horror. '*On her lap?*'

'Why yes!' said the bat. 'He is snuggled up on her knees, underneath her heart, and his white paw is folded round her wrist. It is quite a touching picture to see a poor old lady being comforted by her cat!'

'Old lady? Comforted?' repeated the little wooden horse.

'She looked very sad!' said the bat. 'There were tears on her cheeks as if she had been crying, and the cat's fur was quite damp in patches. I felt quite sorry for her!'

'But did you speak to Gobbolino?' pleaded the little wooden horse.

'Oh I did! I did!' the bat said. 'I flew round him a number of times, woke him up, and gave him your message, but he only shook his head. And when he moved the witch clutched him so tightly in her sleep that he could not have got away if he had tried.'

Panic seized the heart of the little wooden horse.

He hardly heard the bat's plea to occupy the caves now that its mission was done. He left the busy little creatures surging out of the rabbit holes and taking possession of their new homes, while he galloped up the path to the summit as fast as he could go.

CHAPTER 12

THE WITCH FINDS OUT

By the time he arrived at the entrance to the witch's cave the afternoon was nearly over, and the little wooden horse knew it was already too late to begin their journey before nightfall. But in his busy mind a plan was forming. They would go as far as the church in the village that night, and ask the old priest to let them shelter there till dawn. He did not believe the witch would follow them inside the church, and they would wait till she went back to the mountain before they made a run for the stream.

It all depended on rescuing Gobbolino as quickly as possible. He did not believe the bat's tale that his friend

did not want to leave the witch. He was afraid Gobbolino must be under some kind of enchantment, and what it was he would make it his business to find out as fast as he could.

He did not trouble to quieten the noise of his wheels, but galloped up the rough path, kicking stones to left and to right as he ran.

Sure enough, Gobbolino was sitting on the witch's lap, but unlike the witch, he was not asleep. His blue eyes were wide open to welcome the little wooden horse, and a smile of pure joy and surprise spread across his whiskers.

'Oh my friend! My own true and loyal friend!' Gobbolino purred, with tears of joy in his beautiful blue eyes.

He leapt gently to the floor, and licked the little wooden horse all over with a pink and grateful tongue. The sleeping witch made a feeble grab at him, moaned a little and sank into a deeper sleep.

'Come along! Come this instant! We must leave immediately!' said the little wooden horse, for it seemed as if there was nothing to prevent Gobbolino from making his escape that very minute.

'No! no!' said Gobbolino. 'You don't understand, my kind little friend! The poor old lady is breaking her heart at the loss of her own cat, my sister Sootica. If you could have seen her tears you would understand that I can't possibly run away and leave her all alone!'

'So she *knows*?' said the little wooden horse.

'Indeed she does!' said Gobbolino. 'In fact, she recognized me quite quickly, and although she knows I am

no good as a witch's cat I think I was able to give her a little comfort in her grief. If she woke up and found me gone as well I really think she might die of sorrow. She has become so old and frail. She told me herself that she can no longer make any real spells without my sister's help. There is no harm in staying just a short while to comfort her until she gets used to the idea of living without Sootica. *You* go back, my dear friend, and tell my family that I am coming, but that I have had to postpone it for a few days. And if you can find a black cat who is willing to keep a poor old woman company for the rest of her life, then I can leave her with a quiet conscience.'

The little wooden horse's heart was touched, but then he remembered the two anxious homes waiting for them far away in the forest. Uncle Peder would be waking each day with the hope that his little friend would arrive before dark, and the children at the farm would be going to bed in tears every night, because their beloved Gobbolino had neither come back nor sent them any message.

The little wooden horse was standing with bowed head in the middle of the floor when he heard an exclamation, and there was the witch sitting bolt upright on her stool and staring at him.

'And what in the name of all wonders can you be?' she exclaimed in astonishment. 'Did you bring it with you, Gobbolino?'

'Yes, ma'am! ... No, ma'am! ... This is my friend, ma'am!' said Gobbolino in some agitation, for he was not at all sure how the witch would receive the little wooden horse. She might immediately turn him into something dreadful, or simply throw him down the mountainside on to the terrible rocks below.

But she did not seem inclined to touch him. Instead, she got up and walked round and round him as Sootica had done.

'Wooden head! Wooden body! Four wooden legs and wooden wheels!' she chanted. 'What a strange sight to be sure! And do you know my faithless cat, Sootica, my little wooden friend?'

'I met her for the first time last night, ma'am!' replied the little wooden horse quite truthfully.

'Well, well!' the witch repeated, shaking her grey head. 'Kitchen cats and wooden horses in my cave! Here's a pretty kettle of fish!'

The witch was no longer crying, neither did she seem

revengeful or angry. She even seemed to welcome Gobbolino and the little wooden horse. She offered them food, but they were too nervous to eat it, after which she fanned the ashes of the fire under the cauldron into a warm blaze.

'Make yourselves at home!' she told them, agreeably. 'I have to go out for an hour or two, round about the mountainside, but I shall be back before long. If I find my cat Sootica I shall give her the drubbing of her life, but you have been kind and good to me, little Gobbolino, in all my troubles, and I shall not harm you. You won't be lonely with your friend to talk to, and by morning I shall be home.'

She tottered out of the cave into the twilight, dragging her broomstick behind her.

Even the little wooden horse was hesitant to leave after such trust and confidence, and the two of them were glad of the chance to talk together and make a plan for the future.

They lay down together beside the fire, very glad to have one another's company.

'My sister has betrayed *us* too!' Gobbolino said sadly when the witch was gone. 'For she told me for certain the witch would not wake up till sundown, but she did. Only, if I had escaped while she was asleep, as Sootica suggested, just think of the poor old lady waking up all alone! I really can't bear to think of it! Wicked she may have been, but now she is past all that, and what is to become of her?'

'It is just as bad as I said,' the little wooden horse agreed. 'For she brought up your sister, and taught her all she knew, and now Sootica has deserted her. I told her how wrong it was, and she wouldn't listen. But what about your own happy home, Gobbolino? Have you thought about that?'

'Why yes, of course I have!' said Gobbolino. 'And I don't mean to stay here for ever. Just for a day or so, or even less. I must let the witch settle down and get over the shock. Then I will ask her permission to leave, and I will go to find my sister Sootica, who in my opinion is never likely to make a good kitchen cat at her age. She is quite likely to be tired of it already! And do you go home ahead of me first thing in the morning, my dear friend, and I promise to follow you as soon as I can!'

But when the witch came back she was no longer unhappy but chuckling with glee.

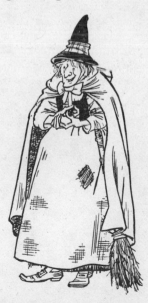

'Nobody can leave me now!' she gloated. 'Nobody can come in or go out! I have painted a magic ring with my broomstick all the way round the foot of the mountain! Down there in the caves the bats are sealed in as tight as little bunnies! The goats on the crest are up there for good, not that the goats want to be anywhere but on the tops of the hills. And nobody can come up the mountain either, unless they have witch's powers or can undo my spell! We will all live happily together, my dear little friends, and nobody shall disturb us ever again!'

'What will happen to anyone who tries to go through the magic ring?' asked Gobbolino, quite horrified.

'They will F R I Z Z L E !' said the witch dramatically 'And nothing will ever be seen of them . . . not ever again!'

CHAPTER 13

THE BOOK OF SPELLS

As daylight faded and the stars came out, the witch's spirits rose and she became more and more vigorous and cheerful. She showed great kindness to Gobbolino and the little wooden horse, and tried to tempt them with all kinds of tasty food which she dished out of her cauldron,

and which immediately turned into anything she asked for.

'A piece of fish, Gobbolino?' and there was a delicious piece of fried fish in the middle of a plate.

'No thank you, ma'am. I am not hungry!'

'Some hay, little horse? Or a juicy carrot? Look! here it is!'

The little wooden horse turned away from the tempting bowl and wished he did not feel so empty inside.

'A piece of sweet cake, Gobbolino? Some corn, or green grass, Dobbin? A little piece of meat dipped in gravy? Look how good it is! I don't like to see you going hungry, my little friends,' the witch said, 'but if you do not want it I shall eat it all myself!'

And she did: fish, corn, hay, meat, cake, grass and carrots, which made Gobbolino certain that there was something very odd in the food that would not have agreed with them at all.

'I am going out for the night on my broomstick!' she told them when her meal was finished. 'I can take either one of you with me. Which of you would like to come?'

But the two friends explained that, since it was their first night on the mountain, whichever of them was left behind in the cavern would be lonely and frightened. Rather reluctantly the witch allowed them to stay together and set out without them.

The moment she was gone Gobbolino seized the milk jug and galloped up the mountain in the moonlight to find the goats, with the little wooden horse close on his heels.

The goats were sleeping. They were not at all ready
to give any of their milk at that hour of night, but when
they understood that the two friends had nothing else
that they dared eat, and were on the point of starving,
they kindly agreed to fill the milk jug, and this time
Gobbolino milked them very nicely indeed.

His paws were soft and kind. The goats liked him,
and asked him to come back in the morning. They also
promised to show him a fine patch of bilberries to eat,
and a wild apple tree sticking out of a rock, with sweet
yellow apples hanging on its branches.

When Gobbolino and the little wooden horse had
both drunk their fill of goats' milk they returned to the

cave. The witch was still absent, flying round and round the stars on her broomstick.

Her book of spells was lying under her bed, and Gobbolino dragged it to a rock, where the moonlight fell on its pages.

Many of the spells looked very disagreeable indeed. There was one which made a heart as cold as ice, for ever and ever. Another caused finger tips to paint every object they touched a horrid shade of green, and a third

was a weeping spell, that made a person cry without ceasing until a fourth spell set him or her laughing again, when they laughed and laughed until they died of exhaustion.

There was a spell for causing the most appalling dreams, and one for creating a voice that croaked like a raven, or hair that stood straight up on end and would never lie down. There were spells that made fingers double their numbers up to ten on each hand, or feet twist and turn so that the owner could only proceed by spinning in giddy circles.

Shocked as they were by these nasty tricks Gobbolino and the little wooden horse were fascinated by the horrid collection, and found themselves unable to put down the book until they had finished it. They could well believe that the witch had the power to encircle the mountain so that no one could escape from it, and before long they arrived at the very page that described the way to do it. She must have known the spell off by heart.

Their own hearts were very heavy, knowing that they were prisoners until the witch chose to let them go. And perhaps she will never let us go at all, thought Gobbolino.

He was about to close the book when some small print at the bottom of the very last page caught his eye. The lines were very narrow and compressed, as if someone had copied them out quite rapidly, without attaching much importance to the message. Even the proper capital letters were missing. The directions read:

'to undo a spell
use clean spring water 8 parts
and clean fresh fruit juice 4 parts
and clean new milk 8 parts
mix all together and stir with a clean left hand
together with the blessing of a good man and five
tears of true sorrow.
splash this on the spell and it shall be broken
pour over the victim and he shall be free.'

The little wooden horse skipped for joy.

'Why! We can make it in a moment and go home directly!' he cried happily.

'Wait! Wait! Don't go so fast!' Gobbolino warned him. 'How are we to collect enough spring water and enough fruit juice, and enough milk to wash away the spell that lies all round the bottom of the mountain? And what about the good man's blessing? And the tears of sorrow, even when we have done all that?'

'Not the *whole* mountain!' said the little wooden horse. 'We only need to break a small part of the circle so that we can escape through it. We had better begin directly!'

'But the blessing! the blessing!' cried Gobbolino. 'There's nobody but ourselves on the whole of this mountain, and there is no way that anybody can come in without being frizzled to bits as he crosses the spell. How can you possibly say we can make it in a minute?'

'I think,' said the little wooden horse seriously, 'that we had better go and ask the bats. You must stay here, since the witch is likely to need you, and I will go down the mountain and see what I can do.'

He set off alone, while Gobbolino set the jug underneath the spring to catch as many drops as he could for the making of the spell-breaker.

The witch came in thirsty and tired, about dawn. She did not notice the absence of the little wooden horse, but drank all the water in the jug, flung her broomstick into one corner and her shoes into another, sat down on her stool and went to sleep.

CHAPTER 14

ASKING THE BATS

As he hurried down the mountainside a plan was form-ing in the head of the little wooden horse.

If the blessing of a good man was needed, who better than the good old priest who had befriended them in the church? And who were better fitted to take a message to him than the bats? Surely they could fly high enough to avoid being frizzled by the spell?

He kept a wary eye for the witch in the sky above, but she was far away on the other side of the mountain.

The bats were busy below, and so happy to have possession of the caves with no one to chase them out that they gave the little wooden horse a warm welcome, and insisted on his coming to inspect one dwelling-place after another. They made him admit that they had the best homes in the world to live in.

'Not that we could go back to the church, even if we wished to,' the bats said, 'because somebody has put a magic circle round the foot of the mountain, and we could not fly through it without being frizzled as we flew. So it is just as well we have somewhere pleasant to make our homes in. The only trouble is that two or three of the younger bats lagged behind, and now they can't join us! They are still living in the rabbit holes outside, and making a great fuss about it.'

The little wooden horse could see a few batlike shapes
whirling and tumbling in the moonlight where the
mountain joined the plain. He walked towards them till
the bats in the caves begged him to stop before he got
frizzled up.

'It is very dangerous over there!' they warned him.

The bats in the rabbit holes caught sight of him and
came fluttering across to see what was happening.

'Ugh! you are scorching!' they cried, retreating a little,
and flopping onto the ground like so many little black
goblins.

'What do you want?' they asked curiously of the little
wooden horse.

'I want to send a message to the old priest in the church. Will you take it for me?' he asked them.

The bats began to twitter.

'We don't want to go back to the church! We want to live in the caves like the rest of our families!' they protested. 'The church is draughty and dirty and everybody hates us there! The priest calls us nasty vermin! The church cleaners detest us! We don't want to go back again!'

'Then why not come and live in the caves with the others?' the little wooden horse said cunningly.

'We will get frizzled up if we try to cross the magic circle!' said all the bats in chorus.

'It's the old witch!' one of the younger ones said. 'She drew a magic circle round the mountain last night with her broomstick. We saw her!'

'But wouldn't you like to find a way of breaking the magic circle?' asked the little wooden horse.

'Oh yes! oh yes! oh yes!' chorused the young bats.

The little wooden horse began to tell them about the spell-breaker – not the whole of it, for fear they might spread the news far and wide until it came back to the witch's ears, but vaguely, and introducing a few ingredients that would serve to put the witch off the scent.

'An owl's feather,' he quoted. 'And a white snail's shell, and a four-leaved clover. But above all, we need the blessing of a good man.'

The bats were silent, looking at him with their bright and beady eyes. They seemed to be considering the subject. At last one piped up:

'But how shall we bring you the blessing if we get it?'

This question had indeed puzzled the little wooden horse, but now he found an answer.

'You must tell the whole story to the priest,' he said, 'tell him about the spell-breaker we are about to make, and explain that his blessing is the most important part of it. You can ask him of his kindness to bless my little wooden ear, and send it back to me. Carry it very carefully between you. It isn't very heavy! Hide it in one of your holes until sundown tomorrow, when I will come and fetch it.'

As he spoke the little wooden horse took off one of his little wooden ears, and threw it as high in the air as he was able, to the bats. It landed, just the slightest bit scorched, on the ground among them.

They picked it up gingerly with the sharp little claws at the end of their wings, and he saw them fly away with it into the darkness of the plain.

When he got back to the cavern the witch was home and fast asleep, while Gobbolino was patiently waiting for him.

CHAPTER 15

THE FLYING HORSE

THE little wooden horse and Gobbolino made up their minds to spend the next day collecting the rest of the ingredients for the spell-breaker.

They found an old pumpkin on a shelf, and this they thought would make a good receptacle for the ingredients, if they could only keep it hidden from the witch.

They pushed it into the very darkest corner of the cavern near the spring, and measured into it the first little clay potful of water, that had collected so slowly from under the dripping rock. They did not like to think how long it would take to collect seven more portions.

In the morning the witch was sleeping so soundly that they hoped she might really sleep all day as Sootica had described to them, and taking the milk jug with them they went out onto the mountainside. Since she knew they could not escape from her, the witch was quite content for them to roam among the rocks outside . . . so long as they came instantly to her bidding when she called them.

Only one thing perplexed them. They were expected to bring back the jug brimming with milk, so how were they going to carry the fruit juice, when they had crushed the bilberries and apples on the rocks and measured them to the right proportions?

Gobbolino brought the little clay cup with him, and suddenly the wooden horse had the good idea of using his hollow wooden body as a mixing bowl, and measuring the ingredients very carefully inside it.

The goats were willing enough to give their milk this morning, but the little wooden horse pointed out that this might go bad in the heat of the sun, and they would be wiser to collect it when they had gathered and crushed the fruit to their needs. Meanwhile, the goats showed them the way to a valley full of bilberries and wild apples, and these they picked and crushed between rocks till the juice ran out.

It took them half the day to crush and collect four measures in the little clay cup, but they were encouraged by finding a spring of fresh water that ran much more freely than the one inside the cavern. They were able to collect all they needed without any trouble, after which it only remained to milk the goats and go back with their work three parts finished.

Leaving the pleasant valley behind them they climbed back towards the summit where the goats had recently been grazing, only to find that the flock had disappeared. After a long search they were discovered on a far-off peak, and Gobbolino and the little wooden horse plodded after them, Gobbolino carrying the milk jug and the cup, while the little horse proceeded very carefully so that he would not spill the precious liquid that

had been measured with such care inside his wooden body, and not a drop of which must be wasted on the ground.

They soon discovered that the goats were playing a game with them.

No sooner did they reach the peak than the whole flock raced back past them bleating derisively. They led them a merry dance over crag and rock and valley before allowing themselves to be caught and milked. They thought it the greatest sport in the world to see Gobbolino and the little wooden horse panting and scrambling after them. They would wait until they were almost within reach and then set off again, leaping and bounding and flicking their tails – their bleating sounding for all the world like mocking laughter. It was as if, having had their milk rejected in the morning, they were now taking their revenge.

In the end real tears of frustration and despair began to flow down the cheeks of Gobbolino and the little wooden horse, and when they saw them crying the goats stopped their teasing and came crowding round them, saying how sorry they were, and trying to make up for their bad behaviour.

Gobbolino was the first to stop crying, for he wanted to milk the goats as soon as possible.

Just at the last moment he remembered to catch in his paw the last five tears shed by the little wooden horse, and drop them into the mixture already floating about inside his little wooden body.

The wooden horse stopped crying at once. He was horrified to think how nearly the precious tears had been wasted.

Gobbolino filled the milk jug when both friends had had a long drink, and the precious cupfuls had been added to the rest. Then they struggled back to the witch's cave, both so tired they could hardly climb over the rough rocks and stones along their way.

Long before they arrived they could hear the witch angrily calling for them. Her spirits and her vigour rose rapidly at the end of the day, and from a sad old woman she became almost the familiar and fierce old witch that Gobbolino used to know.

'Why have you been dawdling out there?' she demanded. 'I could see you half an hour before you arrived! Didn't you hear me calling for you? Why didn't you come running? Tell me! Tell me!'

'I didn't want to spill the milk, ma'am!' Gobbolino explained humbly.

'Pah!' said the witch, taking the jug and tipping a large mouthful down her throat. 'You could have brought it back earlier in the day! Why you have even lost an ear racketing about on the mountain!' she said, turning to the little wooden horse. 'Whoever heard of such carelessness? Now, you have had the whole day to gad about in the hills and tonight one of you *shall* come with me! Which of you is it to be? I think it shall be the little wooden horse! Yes, yes . . . it shall be the little wooden horse!'

'Oh no, ma'am! no, ma'am!' pleaded the little wooden horse in a great fright, for the idea of riding on a broomstick with the precious spell-break still inside him was quite terrifying. He looked round the cavern to see where he could tip the liquid, and saw the pumpkin standing beside the spring.

While the witch fetched her broomstick he trotted into the corner, emptied the pumpkin and tried to pour the mixture in behind her back. Meanwhile Gobbolino managed to slip in between her legs and trip her up, but in getting to her feet she saw what the little wooden horse was doing, and thought, being rather blind, that he was trying to hide from her inside the pumpkin.

Stumbling across the cavern she caught him by the tail, and before he could prevent it half of the precious spell-break was spilled on the floor.

The witch could not see well enough to notice that

the liquid was coloured with fruit juice and pale with
goats' milk. She poked at it with her stick, and then
poked at the pumpkin, which promptly fell over and
emptied out the remains.

'Well, well – we don't need water while we have
milk!' the witch said, limping out of reach of the mixture
on the floor. She let go of the little wooden horse. Both
he and Gobbolino were shedding tears of bitter disappointment, and now there was no mixture to make good
use of them.

'Come along! Jump up behind me, Dobbin!' said the

witch, going to the entrance of the cave and mounting
her broomstick.

Very reluctantly the little wooden horse climbed up
behind her, but the broomstick would not leave the
ground.

'Get off, then!' the witch cried to him, but when he
jumped thankfully to the ground the broomstick stayed
lifeless and inert, though the witch shook it and cursed
at it, and kicked it and finally flung it onto the ground.

Only Gobbolino had noticed that the end of the
broomstick had been resting in a puddle of the nearly-
finished spell-break, the rest of which had now vanished
into the cracks of the cavern floor, taking with it all the
efforts of their long day's work. Even the pumpkin lay
upside down and was drained quite dry.

'If my broomstick will not carry me, perhaps my horse will!' shrieked the witch, leaping onto the back of the little wooden horse.

'Up! Up! Up!' she yelled at him. 'Up to the stars, my horse! Away! Away!'

To the great surprise of the little wooden horse and

the distress of Gobbolino he suddenly found himself rising in the air.

The witch was no great burden, being mostly skin and bone, and the feeling of flight was so delightful he hardly heard his friend's cries.

In fact, it was the witch who was flying, clasping the little wooden horse so tightly with her knees that he felt he himself had wings, and although the effort she put into it was greater than riding on a broomstick, she rose valiantly above the summit of the mountain and sailed away to the north, quite heedless of Gobbolino's pitiful cries below.

The moon shone over the earth with a wide, white radiance, and below him the little wooden horse could overlook a great many miles of country spreading out on every side. He could see the river, and even the faraway forest across the plain, with the village and the church tower standing out clearly in the moonlight. Between the village and the Hurricane Mountains, far, far below them, and not very far out of the village itself, a small dot that might or might not be an animal, or a bird, or even a human being, was wending its way.

And suddenly the little wooden horse realized that the bat might indeed have delivered its message, and the moving dot might even be the old priest answering their plea and coming to help them! It was only an instinct, but it made him aware.

Too late! too late! The little wooden horse groaned aloud as he thought of the wasted spell-break. It was true that the mixture as it stood had had some success

in putting the witch's broomstick out of action, even
without the good man's blessing, but what was the use
of that when not a drop remained to challenge the magic
of the witch's circle?

The flying itself was wonderful.

When he had overcome his fears that the witch would
let go of him, the little wooden horse began to enjoy the
wild ride, the flashing past of countless stars, and, far
away below, the small winking lights of towns and
villages, the gleam of rivers, and the silver spread of the
sea. For a witch that had such a dread of water they
must have crossed a thousand streams.

What he did not know was that at such a height she
might go where she pleased, but she could not descend
to their level. Once she crossed a stream down on the
earth her powers were done.

Round and round the night sky they whirled, and
each time they came within sight of the plain the small
black spot seemed to have moved a little nearer to the
Hurricane Mountains.

The little wooden horse felt sure now that it was the
priest from the church, and his heart ached to think of
the old man's long journey on foot across the plain, by
night, and all alone, when his journey was now quite
useless. Why, oh why, could he not have sent back the
little wooden ear with his blessing on it?

And then he thought: why should not he and Gobbolino make the spell-break again in the morning? But
would the priest wait? There was no shelter on the plain
outside the magic circle, and no human being could

hide in a rabbit hole, like a bat. If the witch saw him he might be running a terrible risk. He did not think that witches cared for priests at all.

As they circled high above the mountains for the fifth time the little wooden horse noticed how the magic circle glowed at night with a fire that was quite invisible by day. It was really very beautiful, and he wished he could show it to Gobbolino waiting so sadly below. He wondered how many more times the witch would fly round the stars, and a dreadful fear crossed his mind that the priest might arrive before morning, quite unaware, and get frizzled up in crossing the magic circle. If only the messenger bat had thought to warn him!

To be sure, he was moving very slowly across the great, empty plain below, but every time he came in sight he was further from the village and nearer to the mountains.

The little wooden horse became agitated by the thought that he would not get back in time to warn the old man of his danger. Then he thought: surely the bats will tell him when he gets there? But bats are so empty-headed, they might not even think of it before it was too late to save his life.

The witch swooped and soared and made tremendous loops around the stars as if she were catching them in an invisible lasso.

'Are you enjoying yourself, my little horse?' she called out to him.

'Oh yes, ma'am,' the little wooden horse replied

politely, 'but I am getting rather tired, ma'am, and I should like to go home!'

'Oh fiddlesticks! we are only halfway through the night!' scoffed the witch. 'My broomstick never got tired or asked to go home. And besides, I am doing all the work! How can you possibly be tired?'

The little wooden horse said nothing. But the next time they flew over the plain it seemed to him that the black speck had moved quite a lot nearer to the foot of the Hurricane Mountains.

'Please, ma'am,' he pleaded, 'I would like to go home now!'

'You would like to go home?' jeered the witch. 'Why, we haven't nearly finished our ride! Wait and see what I can show you! Do you see that great bank of thunderclouds? Have you noticed those lightning flashes? Now watch what we will do with them!'

Gripping the little wooden horse even tighter between her knees she plunged into the mass of tossing thunderclouds, diving in and out of them as if they had been breakers on a sea shore. It was exhilarating, it was exciting. If the little wooden horse had been there of his own accord he would have revelled in the plunging and the tumbling, the diving between flashes of lightning and the witch's wild, triumphant shouts in reply to the pealing of the thunder. He even joined in with a shrill whinny as they chased after the rolling echoes and leapt over the lightning that struck at them like sword-blades.

'There!' yelled the witch. 'I told you that you would enjoy it!'

'Please, ma'am,' said the little wooden horse, 'I should like to go home!'

She only laughed at him as the pair of them were tossed aloft and came streaking down a lightning flash so brilliant it seemed about to cut them in two.

At last even the witch grew tired of the breathtaking game. Her grasp faltered a little, and for an awful moment the little wooden horse thought she might be going to let him go, but she recovered herself, and sailed out of the tumult of the storm into the quieter circle of the night, lit by a thousand stars.

Now, thought the little wooden horse, she is bound to

have had enough of her fun, and we will be able to go back to the cavern.

The moon had vanished behind the clouds at the edge of the storm, but its light still challenged the darkness, and out on the plain the little black speck had nearly reached its goal, although it was difficult to pick it out against the shadows.

In the east, a new and pinkish light was appearing, as morning crept very slowly over the edge of the earth.

'Can we go home now, please, ma'am?' asked the little wooden horse.

He had much better not have spoken, for his request put the witch into a contrary mood.

'Why, it isn't morning yet!' she protested. 'How feeble you are! Why, my cat Sootica and my old broomstick used to fly and fly and fly till the daylight blinded us!'

'I am sorry, ma'am,' said the little wooden horse, 'but please may we go home now?'

'Just one more turn!' said the witch reluctantly. 'And then maybe another . . .'

Away she sailed, round and round the great arches of the sky, and when once more the plain came into sight the little wooden horse could not see anyone on it at all. True, the daylight had come, and all kinds of shadows and rocks were standing up on the earth that might or might not be human beings, but the little wooden horse grew sick at heart when he saw that none of them were moving, as far as his eye could see.

Suddenly, with a magnificent sweep the witch came down on the crest of the Hurricane Mountains, at the same moment as the sun's first rays shot into the sky. Far away in the north the last of the storm died away, and the clouds dispersed. A golden light stole over the land below as the morning came.

They came to rest beside the cavern, and the witch dismounted, staggering inside like a rider aching from long riding and a hard saddle.

'But a wooden horse is better than a broomstick to ride!' she said approvingly. 'I shall have to make a spell to give you flying powers, and we will have some magnificent journeys together!'

She took off her hat and her shoes, sat down on her stool and went almost immediately to sleep.

The little wooden horse ran to awaken Gobbolino, who was fast asleep beside the cauldron.

'Come quickly! Quickly!' said the little wooden horse. 'There is not a moment to be lost!'

CHAPTER 16

SOOTICA ON HER WAY

Two days before this, when the old priest met a little black cat at the door of his house, he thought at first it was Gobbolino, and called to his housekeeper to get a saucer of milk and some other dainties for the little cat to eat.

He was very glad to see it again, and made Sootica very welcome, not least because he thought she had rid the church of the bats that had plagued the congregation for so long. Already the people were coming back to church, and the bells were rung joyously at the proper hours.

Sootica, for her part, had her eye on the tidy warm parsonage, and thought this was not at all a bad place for a cat to make her home. Already the big open world frightened her a little, but the old priest seemed very kind and harmless, while she felt positive her own mistress, the witch, would never dare to come near so holy a place as the church.

While he went to get the milk she sat in the sun washing her face and trying to make up her mind whether she would trouble to go any further when there was such a comfortable place close at hand to live in.

'But where is your friend, the little wooden horse?' the old priest asked her, coming back from the parsonage kitchen.

'Oh, he's still up in the mountain!' said Sootica carelessly.

Hearing her voice, which was rather loud and shrill, the old priest stared at her, and at the same moment the housekeeper appeared, carrying a saucer of milk and a plate full of food that looked very good to eat.

The housekeeper stared too.

'That's not the cat you had before,' she exclaimed. 'I only caught a glimpse of it, to be sure, but I'll swear it had slightly tabby fur and one white paw, and its eyes were blue! Look at this one's feet – black as ink, all of them – and its eyes are green as little apples!'

Sootica looked at her angrily, and sure enough, the flashing of her eyes was a brilliant emerald green.

She opened her mouth to spit, but thought better of it and applied it instead to the good food that the housekeeper had brought for her to eat.

'This is very extraordinary!' said the priest, puzzled. 'Really this cat is very like the other one! Can it be . . . no! it is hardly possible . . . but *is* it the little sister Sootica that Gobbolino talked about? The sister he was going up the Hurricane Mountains to rescue?'

With her mouth full of food and splashes of milk round her chops Sootica mewed agreement. The old priest was more puzzled than ever.

'But what are you doing here without your brother, my young friend?' he asked her.

Sootica merely dipped her nose in the plate and went on eating. She did not intend to begin explaining to these people until she had eaten her fill.

'He was so anxious to save you!' the old priest went on reproachfully. 'I never saw a cat so concerned about his sister! and his wooden friend likewise! I do pray and trust that no harm has come to them in saving you from the witch?'

'Oh none! none!' said Sootica carelessly, licking the last of the gravy from the dish. 'He will be passing by later in the day I do assure you, though it is quite possible he will not have time to pay a call.'

'I am glad to think he will be on his way home,' said the priest, much relieved. 'And tell me, are the bats settled in their new quarters? And are they likely to stop in their homes?'

'Oh positively! positively!' said Sootica, washing away, though not very carefully. 'They have beautiful new homes, and so has my brother Gobbolino, and so has the little wooden horse, and it is their own affair if they don't want to stay there! They all have beautiful new homes to live in except poor little me!'

'That is a sad story!' said the old priest sympathetically. 'Were you so very unhappy up there with the witch?'

'Miserable! Miserable!' said Sootica, although looking back on it the witch's cavern already seemed more attractive than it once had done. The parsonage was almost too clean for comfort. 'I don't know what I shall do now!' she said plaintively, with a final wipe to her chops.

'Why! Perhaps we can find you a small corner in our house!' said the priest happily, but his housekeeper broke in at once.

'That's a witch's cat, your reverence! It's written all over it. You don't want the likes of that in the parsonage, it would be worse than having those nasty bats about the place! Don't you have anything to do with it, your reverence!'

'You rude hag!' said Sootica crossly.

Even the priest was shocked.

'Come! come!' he protested, calming them both. 'After all, the poor puss need not live in the parsonage. She could live in the church – in the vestry, of course – and catch the mice!'

'I don't want to live in the church!' snapped Sootica, who was already trying to remember a spell that would turn the housekeeper into something particularly disagreeable, but there was an atmosphere about the old priest that made her powerless. She sat sulking on the floor and decided to leave as soon as possible.

'Please tell me, little cat, what has become of your brother?' the priest asked her. 'And why are you travelling all alone? I thought he meant to take you back with him to his home in the forest, but that may have been a misunderstanding on my part. Is he still up there on the mountainside? and if so, why?'

'He has taken my place with the witch,' said Sootica calmly. 'As you can see, we are very much alike, and when I left home the witch was asleep! She is getting blind, I don't expect she will notice the difference!'

'Why, you selfish, good-for-nothing little baggage!' cried the housekeeper. 'Do you mean to say you have run away and left your brother to his fate? What will the witch do to him when she finds you have deceived her?'

'If he is lucky she will never find out,' returned Sootica, 'but I think after all I would be wiser to get to the far side of the stream as we planned when I left the cavern, and my brother will follow me at noon. The witch is pretty blind by daylight, and she can't cross water at earth level, as I can, so she is not likely to catch either of us, and as for the little wooden horse, he can look after himself I imagine!'

The priest realized that Sootica was a very different character from her brother Gobbolino.

'You say he will pass by here at midday?' he asked her again.

'Yes. The witch sleeps nearly all day long,' Sootica replied. 'But it was necessary for Gobbolino to stay so that if she did wake she would think it was me. But if I'm not to stay here I must get on and cross over the stream, so I shall be safe. When my brother turns up you will know he is safe too. Tell him I shall not wait for him at the stream after all. We shall no doubt see each other by and by. It will take me all my time to find myself a good home to live in. I am determined to be a proper cat in the future and not a witch's cat any more. At any rate, not often!'

'Much good may it do you!' muttered the house-keeper. She picked up the dishes and took them away to scrub them very thoroughly.

'I hope you find your heart's desire,' said the old priest gravely, opening the door for Sootica to pass out.

She had not been gone more than an hour when the housekeeper came running to the priest in a great state of alarm.

'I told you no good would come of opening the door to that witch's creature,' she cried. 'It has even brought the bats back with it!'

'The bats!' said the priest in dismay. 'What? All of them?'

'Well, one of them at any rate!' said the housekeeper. 'It keeps banging away at my kitchen window and trying to get in. I'm not going to open up to the nasty brute! I'm off to find my brother-in-law to come and shoot it with his gun!'

She was gone before the priest could prevent her, and he made his way to the kitchen in time to see the bat disappearing round the corner of the house.

Later on, as he went to lock up the church for the night, he found the bat flying round and round the bell-ropes, twittering.

To his great surprise, for he had never been very friendly to the bats, the little creature flew down immediately and perched on his shoulder. He could see that it was quite a young bat, and it was carrying something in its sharp little teeth, something wooden and carved, which it now let fall to the floor, as it continued to twitter into his ear.

For a long while the twittering made no sense, and he stooped to pick up the little wooden object and examine it.

It lay flat in the palm of his hand, looking strangely familiar, although he could not for the life of him say what it reminded him of.

And then, in a flash, sudden recognition came to him.

It was the ear of the little wooden horse!

The old priest was horrified. What dreadful adventure had befallen his little friends up there on the Hurricane Mountains? He had not felt happy about them since Gobbolino's sister had appeared in his stead, having escaped so heartlessly without him.

Her story had made him most uneasy. It was all very well to say her brother and the little wooden horse were safe and would soon be on their way home, but what would happen if the witch did, in fact, wake up and find they had deceived her? Sootica would not be there to take the blame, and what dreadful vengeance would she take upon them? Or, what dreadful vengeance had she in fact taken, since here was the little wooden horse's wooden ear lying in his hand, perhaps the only bit of him left? It was too terrible to contemplate.

And then he became aware of the young bat still murmuring and hissing in his ear, and repeating the words: 'Bless it! Bless it! Bless it!' over and over again.

The priest was none the wiser, nor was he at all comforted by the bat's instructions. Yet after all, if his good little friend were dead it was only right and proper to bury his ear with a suitable blessing. He went into the churchyard, still carrying the wooden ear, to get a spade from the toolshed and to find a quiet corner where he might bury it and say a blessing over his humble grave.

The bat became extremely agitated and even aggressive. When the priest tried to brush it away it beat his cheeks with its small wings and even bit the lobe of his ear till blood appeared. All the while it kept up its excited twittering: 'Bless it! Bless it! Bless it!' till it became clear enough to the old priest that it did not intend him to bury the ear first.

Wiping the blood from his own ear he half turned his head towards the little bat and inquired mildly:

'And why are you asking me to bless it?'

This time the bat had some difficulty in getting out the words he wanted to say. After several attempts it stammered:

'Gobbolino!'

Then, delighted at mastering the name, it left his shoulder and flew back into the church, twittering:

'Gobbolino! Gobbolino! Gobbolino!'

The priest followed it, carrying the wooden ear in his hand.

Standing in the nave, he sprinkled the ear with holy water and blessed it, first once, and then twice more, praying that its brave owner might be safe and sound, and find his way home from the witch's territory without harm. The little bat perched on a choir stall, and seemed to take a deep interest in the proceedings.

The priest did not know what to do next. He walked to the door and looked out across the plain. It was past midday, and if Sootica's word could be trusted the little wooden horse and Gobbolino ought to have passed through the village by now. No doubt she herself had already crossed the stream and was well on her way to the forest, or wherever she intended to look for a home.

The priest did not think she would find it very easy to get one.

Perhaps the bat would take the ear back to its owner the way it had come? But the young bat seemed coy, and by its twitterings and mutterings he slowly made out its explanation that it was forbidden to go into the caves on the Hurricane Mountains where its elders had found new homes. It had to be content with living in a rabbit burrow at the foot of the mountain, and it did not want to return there at all. It had decided, it said, to go back to living in the bell tower, where at least it was warm and dry, and it did not get cold and wet at night.

Saying this, it flew swiftly round the church and disappeared above his head into the belfry, through the hole where the ropes hung down.

The priest did not feel inclined to climb the belfry stairs and chase it out. He guessed that, if he did, the bat would simply fly round and round the church and hide somewhere else.

Rather than waste his time on such a wild goose chase he thought it better to go himself to the Hurricane Mountains and find out what was happening, and why it was so important to bless the little wooden ear.

He waited all the afternoon for Gobbolino and the little wooden horse to appear, but when they did not, he carefully locked up the church for the night, and set out across the plain. The housekeeper's brother-in-law, who had seen no sign of the bat in the house, stayed on to keep her company while the priest was out.

The young bat was frightened and lonely, but it hung itself up in a corner of the church and went to sleep.

CHAPTER 17

THE MAGIC CIRCLE

GOBBOLINO and the little wooden horse waited only long enough to hear the first snore from the sleeping witch. Then they fled from the cavern down the mountainside in the first rays of the sun, their hearts throbbing with anxiety.

They fully expected to arrive too late, and to find the good priest had been frizzled up in trying to cross the circle of magic fire. As they ran they met a few late bats, making their way home, and sure enough, some of them flying high had seen the old man advancing across the plain, and these were triumphantly certain that this must have been his fate.

'Yes! We saw him coming! And, yes, it was the priest from the church and none other! And, yes, if he has arrived he has probably been frizzled up by now! And serve him right, the horrid old man! Why couldn't he let us alone? He can't complain about us any more! We aren't going back to his old church ever again! We don't want to! We are quite comfortable where we are, with nobody flapping cloths at us, or shooting us with pellets if we dare to fly about outside! And those horrid, noisy old bells! We couldn't move without their jangling, and whoever wants to hear them again?

'The young ones? Yes, they are grumbling and

complaining outside the magic ring, but there aren't many of them, and they ought to have come in with the rest of us. As far as we can tell they are making themselves some kind of homes in the rabbit burrows. Serve the priest right, we say, if he has met with the fate he deserves! The witch isn't such a tiresome hag as she might seem!'

Gobbolino and the little wooden horse did not stop to listen to them. They were feeling more and more concerned for the old priest, and fairly galloped down the last part of the track, cutting and bruising themselves on the rough stones, and looking always ahead of them, where the pink flames of the magic fire had faded into the daylight and could no longer be seen.

And as they rounded the last corner before the mountain merged into the plain they came suddenly upon the old priest, not fifty yards beyond the rocks; his kind face broke into smiles as he saw them, and he held out his hands in delight at finding them safe and sound.

He was hurrying towards them when Gobbolino and the little wooden horse stopped short in their tracks and screamed at him to stop too, but a crowd of young bats flocked out of the rabbit burrows and twittered round his head.

It seemed at first as if they were warning him of the secret danger lying between him and the mountain, but soon it became apparent that on the contrary they were deafening his ears to the cries of Gobbolino and the little wooden horse. With shrill screams they were reproaching him, and blaming him for their exclusion from the mountain caves, and the homeless plight in which they found themselves. He struggled on, brushing them good-humouredly from his face and head.

'No! no!' Gobbolino cried out to him. 'Don't come any nearer! You will be burned alive!'

'There is a magic circle round the mountain!' the little wooden horse said. 'The witch made it! You mustn't come any closer!'

The priest could hardly hear their warning for the bats that were buzzing around his head.

'Throw us the blessing! Throw us the blessing!' Gobbolino urged. He knew by the warmth under their feet that they were very close to the edge of the spell.

'Throw it high in the air! Throw it very high!' the little wooden horse directed him, as the priest took the ear out of his pocket. He took a step or two forward in order to hurl it towards them.

'No! no!' cried Gobbolino. 'Go back! Go back! You will be frizzled to pieces if you come any nearer! Throw it as high as you can!'

They danced on the edge of the spell while the priest, raising his arm to throw the little wooden ear, brushed away the swarming bats.

A small morning breeze came gusting across the plain, picking up sand and the odd leaf and tossing the priest's cassock about his legs.

He shook his right arm free of the bats.

'Higher! Throw it higher!' called Gobbolino and the little wooden horse.

The bats pettishly lost interest and flew to the ground, where they sat about on the stones like little black goblins.

The priest hurled the wooden ear high into the air.

At the same moment the breeze hurtled round the rocks and snatched up the wooden fragment like a leaf. Up it soared into the sky, turning over and over as if it had been made of paper.

The priest ran after it. Gobbolino and the little wooden horse dashed forward to catch it as it fell. All three collided, and met where the magic circle tinged the earth with a warm, invisible glow.

In this glow they all stood for a moment, one opposite the other, their feet warm, but not uncomfortable – no sign of frizzling, none of burning, though the bats on their stones squeaked with dismay, and the ear of the little wooden horse fell harmlessly to the ground.

The priest stooped down and picked it up. He was now standing inside the ring of magic fire, and he handled with interest the scorched morsel of wood that had been the ear of the little wooden horse.

'I scorched it when I threw it over the circle,' the wooden horse explained. 'I thought it would be completely burnt up!'

Seeing that the three of them were safe, the young bats tried to follow them across the circle, to the mountain. They hoped for the opportunity to find their way into the caves with the rest of their relations, but they very soon retreated, squeaking with pain, as their ears and toes and wings met invisible hot flames, so powerful that one could smell the singeing of their fur.

The hullabaloo they made brought the older bats out of their bedrooms, and a dozen or more came flying from the caverns to find the cause of the commotion.

"Those people went through the magic fire!' the younger bats squeaked, sucking their burnt toes. 'Not

one of them was burnt, not one! But when we tried to follow them we were driven back by the most dreadful flames!'

'Only the perfectly good can go through witches' fire!' said the bats wisely. 'It serves you right! You will just have to go on living outside in the rabbit holes!' and they went back to their caverns.

The younger bats sat down and cried.

The priest, the little wooden horse and Gobbolino looked at each other in perfect astonishment.

'If it is quite true that we can go through unhurt we might just be able to help them,' said the little wooden horse, advancing very cautiously across the warm circle of the magic ring.

'And then we must go home!' said Gobbolino, who could hardly wait to put the Hurricane Mountains far behind him. But he too went forward to help his friend, and the priest did not hesitate to join them.

A dozen bats crowded on to the back of the little wooden horse. More clung to Gobbolino's fur, hiding themselves in the ruff round his neck. The rest crept into the folds of the old priest's cassock.

The little wooden horse put on his ear again.

Together they walked quietly back to the slopes of the mountain, the little bats squealing with joy and gratitude, and praising their rescuers at the tops of their voices.

There was ample room for double their number to

live in the caves, which soon resounded to their chattering and squeaking and their noisy thanks.

The older bats were quite impressed, and sent a delegation to call on the rescuers.

'Thank you for helping our careless children!' they said politely. 'It is more than they deserved, but now they can see for themselves that Good is more powerful than Evil. If we can do anything in our turn to help you, we will be glad to be of service.'

Gobbolino and the little wooden horse remembered how the bats had flown them across the plain from the village, and longed to ask them to do it again. They were both tired and longing to go home, but the bats could hardly carry the priest as well as themselves, besides which Gobbolino could not put out of his mind the sad picture of the old witch waking to find herself alone in the cave at the top of the mountain.

Bad she might be, but she was also a lonely old woman, already deserted by her cat, and now about to be deserted all over again. Yet the old priest and also the little wooden horse had come so far to help him, how could he refuse to go home with them now?

For all he knew, the witch would take the most terrible vengeance on him for the breaking of her spell, and for bringing the priest into her territory. She might throw them all three down the mountainside, and that would be the end of them.

It was thinking of their possible fate that decided him to turn his back on the Hurricane Mountains, and to follow his friends once more across the magic circle and across the plain in the direction of the village.

CHAPTER 18

ESCAPE

As they walked across the plain all three companions became more and more silent.

Gobbolino and the little wooden horse had told their tale to the priest. The priest had told them his. They were all deadly tired, and although Gobbolino had rested all night long in the cavern, it was he who lagged behind the most.

The priest was footsore. The wooden horse was exhausted by circling the stars, and it took all the courage they had to drag their feet one after the other towards the village. They hardly looked behind them as they trudged.

Morning was high in the sky. Breezes and billowing clouds played at shuttlecock over the plain. The spire of the church came nearer and nearer. And Gobbolino fell further and further behind.

The little wooden horse noticed it first, and trotted back to him.

'Are you so tired, my poor little friend?' he exclaimed. 'Climb on my back, and I will carry you. I expect you are much lighter than the witch!'

To his surprise he saw that Gobbolino was crying. Great tears were filling his beautiful blue eyes and falling to the ground.

'Whatever is the matter?' said the little wooden horse, in surprise. 'Surely we are well on our way home now, and so far as I can see nobody is coming after us! Don't be afraid! Ride on my back, and think that this time tomorrow you will be in your own home, and what a welcome will be waiting for you! Can't you imagine it?'

Gobbolino still sobbed quietly, though he cheered up a little as he thought of the children's welcome awaiting him at the farm. It helped him not to dwell on the lonely old witch in her cave, with nobody, *nobody* left to love her! He knew he could never send her another cat to live in such squalor and be her slave. One had to be born to a life like that.

So he refused to ride, and mended his pace till at last they reached the village, and were clasped in the arms of the priest's housekeeper, who could not make enough fuss of them, nor finish stuffing them with all the best food and cream she could find in the parsonage larder.

The priest himself was so exhausted by his double journey that he went to sleep in his chair beside the fire, having first been into the church to say a prayer of thankfulness that his part of the adventure was safely over. He did not care for travelling in witch country at all.

He invited Gobbolino and the little wooden horse to stay the night with him, which they were very glad to do, since the sun was setting and it was still a very long way to reach the stream and safety.

As darkness fell they could see strange lights surrounding the Hurricane Mountains, and tongues of fire flashing up and down again. It all appeared very awesome and rather frightening, but Gobbolino only wept great tears, while the little wooden horse was very solemn. Towards midnight the fires went out.

'All those tears!' said the priest, waking up. 'Tell me, little cat, are you homesick for the old witch up there? Or is it for your family in the forest?'

Gobbolino shook his head, for he really did not know why he was crying.

In the morning his tears were dried, and as soon as it was light he and the little wooden horse said good-bye to their kind friends and set out on the last stage of their journey to the forest.

They were refreshed and well fed by the housekeeper, who could not stop comparing Gobbolino with his sister Sootica – 'that vagabond cat!' as she described her.

Gobbolino, she decided, was a perfect prince of cats, and as good as he was handsome, while as for the little wooden horse, she had never seen such a fine and gentlemanly fellow in all her born days. She stood at the parsonage door beside the old priest, waving to them until her handkerchief became as small as a daisy on the grass of the plain.

The priest had blessed them before their journey, and they trotted along side by side feeling as fresh and as free as the morning itself. The witch's powers seemed so far behind them that they crossed the stream with hardly a thought that she could now no longer harm them.

Gobbolino rode on the horse's saddle, and he swam them both across the water, laughing at the sparkling ripples, and pretending to chase the water-rats that stood

on their hind legs in the entrance to their burrows, most
curious to see such a sight go by.

They clambered up the further bank shaking the
drops of water from their feet and laughing in the sunshine.

'We will be in the forest before sundown,' said the
little wooden horse, 'and I feel fresh enough to trot for a
hundred miles! What about you, my friend?'

'Oh, a thousand miles if necessary!' replied Gobbolino, but he knew that his home was much nearer than that.

Already a distant whiff of pine needles came wafting on the breeze. Home scents and secrets were blotting out the bleak memories of the Hurricane Mountains. Their hearts bounded with happiness.

So it was with a quite unexpected jolt of dismay that a far-off yet familiar sound came to their ears.

Both stopped dead in their tracks to listen.

It now seemed weeks, even months ago that they had been crossing the plain to the sound of just this same dreadful music – the cry of hounds, far off, but coming nearer . . . in pursuit of . . . what?

Without hesitation they turned round and hurried back to the stream. Better to hide for a while among the rocks and rushes than be caught out on the open plain. For the hounds were running between them and the forest, and although at times they seemed to be heading in the opposite direction, at others they turned about, and it was obvious that they were coming closer and closer.

There was a cluster of rocks in the middle of the stream, and to these rocks the little wooden horse waded with Gobbolino on his back. They thought that if they could wait there for an hour or so with the water all round them, the pack might not find their scent, and they crouched in the stones and the sparse scrub that grew round about them, hoping against hope that the hounds might pass by on the far side of the stream without seeing them.

But soon it became quite apparent that they were actually coming up the stream itself, and in the not-so-far distance they could hear the baying and the howls and barking of many dogs, now casting about with muted yelps and whimpers, now in full cry tearing up the shallow places or plunging and splashing in the deep pools of the stream.

What they were actually chasing the two friends could not tell. They only knew that they were in great danger, and that the forest side of the stream was more dangerous than the other.

When the pack was almost within sight they burst out of their hiding-place and splashed to the bank, scrambled up the side of it, over the top, and away across the plain in the direction of the Hurricane Mountains, back over the weary distance they had come, panting, gasping, limping, never pausing or looking behind them,

while the great open spaces around them felt even more dangerous than the hounds.

At any moment they expected the pack to pick up their scent and pursue them, and once they did this there would be no chance of escape. So they ran and ran and ran, not looking for any landmark or direction, while first the afternoon and then the evening closed in around them.

They might have found refuge in the church, but they left it far away to the right of them. The mountains came nearer and nearer, but they did not look up to see them.

Far behind them came that terrible baying, and it continued to pursue them in imagination long after the hounds had given up their quarry and gone home to bed.

They never noticed that in the darkness the magic fire round the mountain no longer glowed. Utterly spent, and more dead than alive they stumbled from the plain on to the rocks. Flinging themselves down in the first cave they found, they fell into an exhausted sleep.

When they woke up it was daylight, and the bats who lived in that cave were twittering about them.

'Why have you come back? Where is the priest? We thought you wanted to go home! What is the matter with you?'

They questioned them over and over again.

Gobbolino and the little wooden horse were too tired and unhappy to answer them at first. As they opened their eyes they remembered they were back again in the witch's country, and between them and their homes were the terrible hounds. There was only the remotest chance that they would ever get back again without losing their lives.

They did notice, however, that the bats were no longer confined to the caves. They were flitting on and off the mountain, back to the plain and back again, as if all the world were theirs and there had never been a magic fire at all.

'Aren't you afraid of burning your wings?' the little wooden horse asked them.

'Oh pooh no! The witch is finished!' scoffed the bats. 'When she knew that you were gone she took a fit and fell down screaming! She is probably dead by now!' they added complacently.

Gobbolino and the little wooden horse sprang to their feet. They left the cave and galloped up the mountainside as if they had never made the long journey across the plain the day before. No matter that their feet were blistered and sore. They did not stop until they reached the crest of the mountain and burst into the cave.

It was as still as a tomb and very cold, since even the ashes under the cauldron were dead and finished.

At first they thought the cavern was empty, and the witch must be out on the mountainside. But her broomstick was in its place, and her shoes thrown one after another into a corner. Her pointed hat lay on the floor. The water still dripped sluggishly from the spring in the rock. It was the only sound in the whole cave.

They were about to go outside and question the goats when in the shadows something moved.

What they had taken for a heap of old rags proved to

have wizened arms and legs, bare feet and a head. The head was crowned with long black hair, out of which peered a long, sad, pale face. They had to stare hard at it to recognize the witch.

As they stared at her the witch's eyes came open, and for a moment she seemed to recognize them. She held out a claw-like hand towards them, and then sank back with a heartbroken sob.

Gobbolino crept up to her and licked her shrivelled face.

'Go and get milk from the goats,' he told the little wooden horse, 'and I will fetch her some honey! Then we will light the fire and make her warm again.'

They flew to fetch honey and some goats' milk.

While Gobbolino fed her spoonful by spoonful, the little wooden horse lit the fire. By the time the cave was warm again and full of pink light and dancing shadows the old woman was sitting up and panting a little as she watched them with tears of gratitude running down her cheeks.

'To meet with such kindness! To have such goodness shown to a wicked old woman like me!' she muttered. 'And I thought I was to be left alone for ever and ever! But these two cared for me after all! These two came back to look after me when all the world had left me alone. I was going to die of loneliness and a broken heart, but now I shall get better. I shall never be lonely any more!'

Gobbolino and the little wooden horse looked at each other in some anxiety at these words, but for the moment the witch's comfort was all their concern. They dressed her and combed her hair, and washed her hands and feet.

When she was clean and tidy she looked quite respectable. As she smiled at them, and thanked them from the bottom of her heart she looked, just for a moment, like a pretty old lady.

As before, her spirits improved as the day went on, and by evening she was almost lively.

The little wooden horse was afraid that she might want to go riding again, but to his great relief she did not suggest it.

Instead, she got out her book of spells and drew her stool up close to the fire.

'Your eyes are better than mine, my dear!' she said to Gobbolino. 'I want to make a spell . . . just a little spell, so that you and your friend will be happy here with me, and not want to leave me ever again! I will make just a little spell so that we shall all three live in comfort in this cave of mine for ever and ever and ever!'

But as Gobbolino opened his mouth in a pitiful miaow of protest there came an answering miaow from the door of the cave.

All three looked up startled, to see the shape of a black cat standing in the doorway. And it was Sootica!

CHAPTER 19

THE LAST SPELL

THE witch uttered one shriek of joy.

Sootica uttered another.

The next moment they were in each other's arms, and purrs, cluckings and endearments mingled so thickly together that it was difficult to distinguish witch from cat or cat from witch.

'Is it really you, my little cat?' cried the witch, when the first excitement of their meeting had died down.

'Yes it's really me! Me! ME!' shrieked Sootica. 'And is it really you, my dear mistress? So thin! So old and pale! Hardly a witch any longer!'

'I don't want to be a witch any more!' said the old witch, wildly swinging Sootica round by the tail, which she did not seem to mind at all. 'All I want is a little company, a little love and affection, and a nice warm cavern to live in for ever and ever! I don't like the outside world at all!'

'Why, you sound just like my brother Gobbolino!' said Sootica, still licking the witch's chin, when she could get a perch on her shoulder. 'And the strange thing is that all I want is just exactly the same thing! I had a dreadful time out in the wide world, trying to find a comfortable home to live in! Nobody wanted a witch's cat like me! The more I promised to be good the less they trusted me. I've been turned out of doors with a boot behind me, or a broom, or a bucket of water! You have no idea how cruel people are out there in the places where people live and work and call themselves human beings. Mind you, nobody got away with treating me like that! The person who kicked me found the sole of his boot dropped off when he next set out from home! And all the bristles fell out of the broom! It was almost new, too! As for the pail of water, there is such a hole in the bottom now it will never hold water again! Serve them all right!'

Gobbolino stared at his sister with his beautiful blue

eyes. It did not sound as if Sootica had altered her character very much since she went away.

She noticed him at last.

'So you are still here, brother, are you?' she said, fixing him with an impudent stare. 'And your wooden friend with you! Are you sorry I have come back? Have you enjoyed being a witch's cat after all?'

The witch seized her by the scruff of her neck and shook her soundly.

'You wicked little wretch!' she cried indignantly. 'Don't you know I nearly died of grief when I found you had deserted me? If it hadn't been for your good little brother and his friend I would have been dead by now! *They* looked after me! *They* cared for me! *They* nursed me back to life! Get into your corner, miss, and count your blessings, for you may well find yourself shrivelled into a hazelnut in return for your heartless behaviour. I don't need your companionship now! These good friends have come to live with me for ever, and I shall reward them as they deserve. Tell me, Gobbolino, my good cat, and tell me, my little horse, now that I have my Sootica back to help me read my book of spells, I can grant you any wish you may utter. What would you like me to do for you?'

Both Gobbolino and the little wooden horse announced in the same breath:

'Please, ma'am! We would like to go home!'

The witch's face fell, but Sootica cackled with laughter, and immediately dashed for the book of spells and began to turn the pages.

'Let them go! Let them go!' she babbled. 'Who wants to keep them?'

'Only, when we were crossing the plain, the hounds chased us!' said the little wooden horse.

'They chased me too,' boasted Sootica, 'but I was too quick for them!'

'The bats might carry us back again!' Gobbolino said hopefully.

'Or my mistress might carry you on her broomstick!' said Sootica.

But the witch closed her lips angrily and shook her head.

'Two would be too heavy, and my stick won't fly these days!' she muttered. 'They put a kind of spell on it and it has never been the same since. Besides . . .' she began to sob, 'if these two go home and leave me, how am I to know that you will stay with me and not desert me for a second time? What is to prevent you from flying off again one morning and never coming back?'

'Oh no I shan't!' said Sootica decidedly. 'I shall stay here for ever and be just a common cat for the rest of my days.'

'Do you promise that?' asked the little wooden horse.

'I promise,' said Sootica.

'No more making of wicked spells?'

'No more . . . not ever.'

'Promise?'

'I promise.'

'Cross your heart?' said the little wooden horse. 'No, cross my ear! The old priest blessed it, so you must swear on my wooden ear that you will never be a witch's cat again.'

'I promise! Oh, I promise!' agreed Sootica. 'And my mistress must promise never again to be a witch.'

'I promise too!' said the witch.

'Will you swear it on my wooden ear?' said the little wooden horse.

'Oh I will, I will!'

The little wooden horse took off his charred wooden ear.

'But how are we going to get home?' asked Gobbolino. 'Supposing the bats won't take us?'

'Wait!' said the witch. 'Before we swear these very important things on the wooden ear, let me make just one more spell. Just one little one!'

Gobbolino and the little wooden horse jumped to their feet in a fright. They did not trust the witch's spells at all. She was whispering now to Sootica, but they could not hear a word that she said.

Sootica smiled and nodded her head. She began feverishly to turn over the pages of the book of spells with her paw.

'No thank you,' Gobbolino said, edging towards the door of the cavern. 'I think we will start on our journey now! We wish you well, ma'am, and you too, sister Sootica, but it is time that we went on our own way.'

Secretly, he felt more ready to face the dangers of the long journey than to risk another moment or another spell in the cavern of the witch.

But both Sootica and her mistress were searching the

pages with excited smiles on their faces, and uttering little cries of delight when they seemed close to finding what they wanted.

'Here it is! No here! Not quite! Two pages further on!'

It could only be a trick to keep them longer in the cave. The little wooden horse stooped down to pick up his ear, and trotted after Gobbolino to the entrance.

'Wait! Wait!' cried the witch. 'Don't be afraid! We aren't going to harm you! We only mean to wish you well! Quickly, Sootica! Get the cauldron ready! Put in this! ... and this! ... and that! Don't lose a moment!'

At these words the little wooden horse and Gobbolino fairly bolted out of the door. The little wooden horse dropped his ear in the entrance but dared not stop to pick it up. 'Uncle Peder will make me another one if I ever get safely back to him again!' he panted.

They hurtled down the path which zig-zagged down the crags in a precipitous fashion. It was so steep, in fact, that when the witch and Sootica appeared from the cave, they were actually directly over their heads, high above them.

'Stop! Wait!' the witch shrieked, hurling something from a wooden ladle that fell like rain down the rocks, in a thousand rainbow-coloured drops.

As he galloped along the little wooden horse received a full dollop on his back, and all at once a most extraordinary sensation filled his body.

He found himself lifting his feet and his wheels from the path. The stones no longer bruised his feet. His wheels, that were wearing out, shed no splinters. He was beginning to fly!

'Gobbolino! Jump on my back! Quickly! Quickly!' he called to the cat scampering on ahead.

Gobbolino stopped, turned round, and leapt in one great bound on to his back.

As he did so the little wooden horse soared into the air . . . higher, higher, and still higher . . .

Now they were on a level with the witch and Sootica who laughed and waved their hands to them from the door of the cavern. The goats, grazing on the rocks, raised their heads and bleated in admiration.

'Good-bye! Good-bye!' called Sootica and the witch, as the wooden horse veered away towards the south.

'We promise!' they shouted after the flying pair. 'We promise! Good-bye! Good-bye!'

'My ear is there to make sure they keep their promise!' the little wooden horse said, flying steadily southwards. 'If they try to throw it away it will burn their fingers far, far worse than the flames in the magic circle.'

'How do you know?' asked Gobbolino.

'I just do!' said the little wooden horse solemnly.

They flew high over the church, where the bells were ringing for service. They would have liked to go down and say a last good-bye to the old priest and his housekeeper, but they did not know how long the spell would last, and if it came to an end in the middle of the plain they would be worse off than before.

So they flew over the steeple, and on across the stream, and now the forest was a dark shadow on the horizon, while down below the pack of hounds were quartering the plain, just as they had done the day before.

Safe as they were at such a height, neither of them could repress a shudder as the dreadful music came to their ears, but soon it was lost far behind them.

'Are you tired?' Gobbolino asked the little wooden horse, as he thought he felt him falter.

'Not exactly,' said the little wooden horse, 'but I think the spell may be coming to an end, because I can't fly quite as high as I did at first.'

'Well, never mind,' said Gobbolino comfortingly, 'because we are very nearly at the forest!'

It was quite true. The trees, that for a long time had been only a far shadow, were now just a short distance below them, and as the flying powers of the little wooden horse slowly faded, they floated lower and lower towards the upraised branches, coming gently to earth at the foot of a pine-tree, and landing on a bed of pine needles that felt as soft as feathers after the rigours of the mountain.

Gobbolino jumped to the ground.

'Do you think you will be able to fly again?' he asked the little wooden horse.

'No, never! Never, never!' said the little wooden horse, and he sounded perfectly satisfied.

It had been a lovely flight. Twice in his life he had soared in the sky, and seen the earth like a carpet spread out below him, but his wooden wheels were not made for sweeping the stars, and he was glad to be down on the earth again.

They decided to spend the night just where they were, and after a little searching they discovered a tree with branches that gave them protection like a kind of tent.

They were just settling down to sleep until the morning when a movement in the branches above them caught their attention.

Not ten feet above their heads sat the owl!

CHAPTER 20

GOING HOME

IT was the same owl that had brought Sootica's message to Gobbolino. He recognized it at once.

The owl made no sign of recognition, but it stared and stared at Gobbolino with its golden eyes, till, finding itself an object of curiosity to the pair of them, it turned its back, but before long it was twisting its head round on its shoulder and staring at them again.

'Oh owl! owl!' Gobbolino cried. 'If you are the same owl, and I know you are, will you please take a message back to our homes in the forest? Oh please, please do!'

The owl immediately rose several feet into the air on wide, soft wings, and came down facing them again. It ducked its head forward, and appeared perfectly willing to be made use of.

Gobbolino looked frantically for something that would do to write a message on, and finally a wide leaf beside the stream seemed large and strong enough to serve for a writing pad. The little wooden horse fetched another.

Side by side on a flat stone Gobbolino scratched the words on each leaf with his sharpest claw:

'WE ARE COMING HOME!'

The owl stretched out its head, flew down, and with a gentle beak received both the messages, transferring them to its powerful claws. Then, without a word it flew off into the darkness, leaving Gobbolino and the little wooden horse greatly comforted. They lay down side by side and slept till morning.

As the sun rose they saw that the owl was back again. He looked very tired, and he was fast asleep with his head tucked underneath his wing.

Before leaving, they thanked and embraced him.

The owl did not open his eyes, but they felt by the fluffing of his feathers that he was pleased by their gratitude.

Far, far away across the plain behind them the pale blue outline of the Hurricane Mountains seemed a

hundred years ago, soon to be swallowed up by the trees of the forest.

They were going home!

Steadily, silently, walking on soft needles instead of stones, they padded on their way, hardly talking now, because their thoughts were all of home.

They knew that they would miss their close companionship when the time came to part. They had not been friends and gone through so many adventures together for nothing. Gobbolino would never forget the loyalty and courage of his friend, the little wooden horse, who had dared so much for him, and risked losing his own life for Gobbolino's sake.

But although the forest was wide, they did not live so very far from one another, and surely there would be days when they could meet and talk over their adventures? Surely the farm children would welcome the little wooden horse with great joy and delight in the farm kitchen? And perhaps Uncle Peder and his wife would be glad to see Gobbolino at their home in the forest when he came to call?

The thought of home was warm and comforting all through the long day's travelling, when the forest trees seemed never ending, and the path was so full of turnings and corners it seemed that it would never arrive anywhere at all.

As morning merged into afternoon and afternoon into twilight they began to think they would have to spend yet another night sleeping out of doors.

In spite of the soft ground their paws and wheels were sore and very weary, and they were walking more and more slowly when far away through the forest a sound made their ears prick, and they stopped all of a sudden in their tracks.

This time it was not the cry of hounds, nor the twittering of bats, nor the far-off, familiar shrieking of the witch. It was music . . . children's voices singing in the twilight . . . singing bravely and loudly to banish the terrors of the darkness, and with them a deeper, bolder voice was joining in the chorus to cheer them on.

Gobbolino gave a little miaow of excitement, while the wooden horse bounded forward with a whinny of joy.

Down the darkening path they galloped, never stopping for a moment until they were in the loving arms of the farm children, who, hand in hand with Uncle Peder,

had braved the dark night and the shadows to come and meet them and take them home.

When their rapturous welcome was over they set off by the way they had come, only calling in for a brief visit to Uncle Peder's home to assure his wife that all was well, and he and the little wooden horse would be with her once they had taken the farm children and Gobbolino safely home.

This being done, the walk back to the cottage from the farm was the happiest moment of the little wooden horse's life.

Telling the story to his master he trotted by his side, with his one ear brushing Uncle Peder's trouser leg, and another ear already promised for the morrow.

He had left his friend Gobbolino purring by the fire, the centre of everyone's love and attention. They had promised to meet one another at the very earliest opportunity. It might even be tomorrow!

And now with his task successfully ended and his adventure over he was going back with his beloved master to his own place by the fire, in that home which he knew was his for ever and ever and ever.